Praise for St. Ursula

"Raine is at once rea_____
find her place in the world, and a very old soul learning
to plant itself in a new generation. *St. Ursula's* reminds
us that it is possible to be gentle guides, who learn
by listening and mentoring, and who rediscover
ourselves along the way."
—*Vermont Woman*

"Raine [has] a precocious adolescent voice that's
reminiscent of Holden Caulfield."
—*Booklist*

"*St. Ursula's Girls Against the Atomic Bomb* [features] an
insatiably curious, stunningly perceptive, irrepressible
young heroine set loose in Manhattan. Each page
shimmers with idiosyncratic beauty and compassion."
—Gayle Brandeis, author of *The Book of Dead Birds,*
winner of the Bellweather Prize for Fiction in Support
of a Literature of Social Change

"So few novels feed us what so many of us hunger for . . .
Hurley has given us a divine gift with this novel."
—Tom Paine, author of *Scar Vegas* and *The Pearl of Kuwait*

Valerie Hurley won the *Indiana Review* Fiction Prize, and
has published stories in *The Iowa Review, The Missouri
Review, The North American Review,* and *New Letters,* among
others. Two of her essays have appeared in *The Best American
Essays* anthologies. She lives in Vermont with her husband.

St. Ursula's Girls Against the Atomic Bomb

ST. URSULA'S GIRLS AGAINST THE ATOMIC BOMB

a novel by Valerie Hurley

A PLUME BOOK

PLUME
Published by the Penguin Group
Penguin Group (USA) Inc., 375 Hudson Street, New York, New York 10014, USA
Penguin Group (Canada), 10 Alcorn Avenue, Toronto, Ontario M4V 3B2, Canada (a division of
Pearson Penguin Canada Inc.)
Penguin Books Ltd., 80 Strand, London WC2R 0RL, England
Penguin Ireland, 25 St. Stephen's Green, Dublin 2, Ireland (a division of Penguin Books Ltd.)
Penguin Group (Australia), 250 Camberwell Road, Camberwell, Victoria 3124, Australia (a division of
Pearson Australia Group Pty. Ltd.)
Penguin Books India Pvt. Ltd., 11 Community Centre, Panchsheel Park, New Delhi - 110 017, India
Penguin Group (NZ), Cnr Airborne and Rosedale Roads, Albany, Auckland 1310, New Zealand (a
division of Pearson New Zealand Ltd.)
Penguin Books (South Africa) (Pty.) Ltd., 24 Sturdee Avenue, Rosebank, Johannesburg 2196, South Africa

Penguin Books Ltd., Registered Offices: 80 Strand, London WC2R 0RL, England

Published by Plume, a member of Penguin Group (USA) Inc. This is an authorized reprint of a hard-
cover edition published by MacAdam/Cage. For information address MacAdam/Cage, 155 Sansome
Street, Suite 550, San Francisco, California 94104.

First Plume Printing, December 2004
10 9 8 7 6 5 4 3 2 1

Parts of this book have been published in slightly different form by *New Letters, Boston Review,* and *The
North American Review.*

Grateful acknowledgment is made to HarperCollins Publishers for permission to reprint a portion of
Sonnets to Orpheus by Rainer Maria Rilke, from *Poems of Rainer Maria Rilke: A Translation from German
and Commentary* by Robert Bly.

Grateful acknowledgment is made to Russell Schweickart for permission to reprint material from his
essay "Our Backs Against the Bomb, Our Eyes on the Stars."

 REGISTERED TRADEMARK—MARCA REGISTRADA

The Library of Congress has catalogued the MacAdam/Cage edition as follows:

Hurley, Valerie
  St. Ursula's girls against the atomic bomb / by Valerie Hurley.
    p. cm.
ISBN 1-931561-55-9 (hc.)
ISBN 0-452-28569-0 (pbk.)
1.Teenage girls—Fiction. 2. Catholic schools—Fiction. 3. Social reformers—Fiction. 4. Student
counselors—Fiction. 5. High school students—Fiction. 6. Manhattan (New York, N.Y.)—Fiction.
I. Title.

PS3608.U77S7 2003
813'.6—dc22   2003014403

Printed in the United States of America

PUBLISHER'S NOTE
This is a work of fiction. Names, characters, places, and incidents either are the product of the author's
imagination or are used fictitiously, and any resemblance to actual persons, living or dead, business
establishments, events, or locales is entirely coincidental.

For John,

my extraordinary husband,

with love and gratitude

It was a girl, really—there is a double joy

Of poetry and music that she came from—

And I could see her glowing

Through her spring clothes:

She made a place to sleep inside my ear.

—Rainer Maria Rilke

St. Ursula's
Girls Against
the Atomic Bomb

Her mother played the violin, her father gazed at stars. Behind their townhouse on West 88th Street was a garden filled with blue jays and purple finches, and from his third-floor window, Al could see the pink roses tumbling over the fence, the orange nasturtiums, the daisies and snapdragons, the yellow-throated Chinese lilies.

For years, he had watched the housekeeper open the window and shake out the scatter rugs and dust rags, the gardener clipping rosebushes, the mother practicing her violin behind the sheer curtain of a second-floor window. The girl was a stranger to him, although he had often seen her in the garden, playing her bagpipes or lying in the hammock. Now he would be working with her, but he did not feel up to the assignment. Even from a distance, there was about her an aura of havoc, disorder, mayhem.

After so many years at his job, he felt more and more reluctant to put on his tie and tweed sport jacket each morning and walk the ten blocks to St. Ursula's Academy, a patrician mansion overlooking the Hudson River. He longed to sit all day and listen for the songs of the bluebird and the yellow warbler. White chrysanthemums, violin sonatas, vines of bittersweet. He wandered into his den early in the morning and watched the birds for half an hour—his favorite part of the day. Then he and Frieda sat in the kitchen by the window, reading *The New York Times* and drinking coffee out of pale china cups. Frieda's tousled hair glistened with currents of red as she sat at the table in her flamingo-pink robe. He thought of buying her a dozen roses and propping them up over the lintel so they floated down over her as she walked through the door. He wanted to be dashing, romantic, courtly. Then perhaps she'd talk about him the way she talked about Daniel Wadhams.

In the afternoons after work, he returned to their quiet apartment, poured himself a Scotch or two, and was snoring in their bed at midnight when Frieda returned from her work as a nurse at the Harlem Home for the Elderly. Before dozing off, he often relaxed by reading about the Middle Ages, a time when the catastrophes— floods, pestilence, and famine—were comprehensible and the news traveled slowly, transmitted by pilgrims, peddlers, and beggars. He imagined pastry cooks shaping dough into the Holy Trinity surrounded by choirs of angels. He imagined the knight falling madly and purely in love.

He had recently discovered *The Thirty-One Rules of Love*, written in the thirteenth century by Andreas Capellanus. His favorite rules were, *Love is always growing or diminishing; Love is always banished from the home of avarice; A love divulged rarely lasts; Every lover grows pale at the sight of the beloved.* His least favorite rule was, *If love grows less, its decline is swift and it seldom recovers.*

* *

On Saturday morning, Al poured their coffee at the kitchen table and watched Frieda reading the newspaper. He had no interest in doing anything. He opened the window. The sky was blue and cloudless, the air warm. The Rassaby girl was lying in her hammock, singing.

Saturday mornings often reminded him of Mrs. Cobelle's—the boarding house in Brooklyn where he had lived with his mother until he had been taken into state custody as a teenager. He remembered his mother disappearing for three or four days, then appearing at the kitchen door one morning as Mrs. Cobelle was flipping bacon in her huge iron skillet and dropping eggs into the sputtering fat. Mrs. Cobelle was always telling him to straighten up and fly right.

Feeling drawn to the girl's singing, Al called goodbye to Frieda and ran down the three flights of stairs, then went around to the back of the building and over to the wrought-iron fence surrounding the Rassabys' garden. Raine was lying in the hammock, singing—

Oh, we'll all go together when it comes,

Oh, we'll all go together when it comes,

Oh, we'll all go together, no matter what the weather,

Oh, we'll all go together when it comes.

"Miss Rassaby?" he said. "Welcome to St. Ursula's Academy. I'm Al Klepatar, your new guidance counselor."

She jumped out of the hammock and reached over the fence to shake his hand. "I've seen you at school," she said. "It's nice to meet you. This is my second try at senior year." She had woolly golden hair, a thin, sharp face, and gray eyes streaked with lavender. She reminded him of a loon. She was wearing pajama bottoms and a blue T-shirt that said, *Better Active Today than Radioactive Tomorrow.*

"I just came to say hello," he said. "We're neighbors. I live over there. I'm surprised you recognize me."

She laughed. "You're the only man in the school, Mr. K."

"I guess we'll be getting to know each other. The Mother Superior wants me to see you twice a week."

"I know. She told me. Do you want to come in?"

"I'm going running. Thanks anyway."

"You're a runner?"

"Yes," he said. "As of today."

"I never do anything ambitious like running, but some-times I walk the sixty blocks down to my grandmother's on 29th Street. Have you looked at my school records? Kind of pathetic, aren't they?"

He smiled. "You could say there's room for improve-ment," he said. "Well, I just wanted to say hi. I should go. I was thinking of going up to Broadway and getting my wife some flowers."

"My boyfriend never gives me flowers or anything else except maybe some mushrooms he finds in the woods. And once he gave me a bird with a broken wing. But it isn't really flowers and candlelight and love songs that are romantic. You know what I think is romantic? Being deeply understood by another person." He saw that a branch of yellow snapdragons was wound through her hair. "My father calls me the awfulizer," she said. "My mother calls me the instigator. I have a pretty good idea of what I want to do with my life, but it isn't exactly what they have in mind."

"Well, we can talk about all this next week," he said.

"I don't think my mother has any hope whatsoever for me, but my father wants me to be an astronaut—or he did." She laughed. "He sent me to space camp in Huntsville, Alabama, every summer, starting when I was nine. For five and a half days, I went around in a helmet and boots and gloves and puffy white leggings and a white shirt with plastic shoulder pads. I learned about payloads and propulsion systems. Actual astronauts came to talk to us. I rode in this machine called 5DF—five degrees of freedom. Sometimes I got to yell into a microphone '10 - 9 - 8 - 7 - 6 - 5 - 4 - 3 - 2 - 1 - BLASTOFF!'"

"What *do* you want to do with your life?" he said.

"Rid the world of nuclear weapons."

"That's an ambitious goal."

"Yeah. I figure it's me or them."

"When I was a kid, we had air raid drills in school," he said. "Then the Cold War warmed up, and they started calling them tornado drills."

"I loved it when Wonder Woman knocked the warhead off a nuclear missile with her tiara. My boyfriend and I like that saying that the best way to make your dreams come true is to wake up."

"Your bagpipes wake me up," he said. "Every Sunday morning."

"I'm sorry. A lot of people complain about my bagpipes. Mary says they live in the noisiest city in the country, but they only complain about the noise when I play my bagpipes."

"Who's Mary?" he said.

"She's our housekeeper. And she's my best friend. Right now, she's standing behind that curtain, watching us. I wish you could meet her, but Mary doesn't act like herself when other people are around. She's from Greenland. She and I share the same religion—the religion of fear. It's embedded in our bones. We always carry around amulets to appease the evil spirits."

"I'm sure you'll make some friends at St. Ursula's."

"I doubt it," she said. "I talked to one girl about the Holocaust, and she thought it was one of the Jewish holidays."

"Well, I'll look forward to getting to know you, Raine. You seem to have a lot to say."

A chartreuse caterpillar was crawling up her sleeve.

"Listen to my horoscope," she said, reaching into the pocket of her striped pajamas. "'Even the most linear thinkers will yield to creative ways to express their adoration tonight.' That sounds hopeful."

"I love your flowers," he said. "Your garden reminds me of the farm where I lived as a teenager."

"You lived on a farm?"

"Yes," he said. "It's up in Putnam County. It's an old rundown place. My grandmother used to put out the cabbage plants when the moon was one-third full. Do you think you could stop in to make an appointment with me on Monday, Raine?"

"Sure," she said. "Where are you going?"

"I promised myself a nap."

"I thought you were going running. You're probably just like me—I want to train for the marathon, but I'm usually heading for the hammock with a bag of Fritos. Right?"

"Right," he said, laughing, and he could feel a buoyancy in his step as he headed back up the stairs to Frieda.

* *

Each weekday morning, Al walked through the hallways decorated with crucifixes and paintings of St. Ursula and the Blessed Virgin and entered his small basement office. The stone wall under the window glittered with mica. Throughout the day, students drifted in and out of the room. Each girl sat down in the blue plastic chair across from his desk and fidgeted, wanting something from him. The girl talked, he talked, the radiator clanked. The

Mother Superior's voice crackled over the loudspeaker. Outside the window, sirens squealed. He imagined the chaos of the universe, the confusion, the longing for order. On damp days, a black mold crept out of the gray stone, drying in the sunlight to a sinister black fuzz.

"Know what my horoscope for the day is?" Raine said, dropping her backpack on the floor and reading to him from a scrap of newspaper. "'You are on a winning streak when it comes to love, but don't push your luck. It's hard to get down to work with your mind buzzing. Patience is a virtue only up to a point. It could be time to stand up for yourself.'"

"That's probably good advice," he said.

Filmy insects were circling the plant on his desk, their crystal wings fluttering in the lamplight. She was sitting across the desk from him in her St. Ursula's jumper and white blouse, a silver star of David hanging around her neck.

A star of David? He leaned back in his chair and listened to what sounded like a very made-up family history—a mother who was born in Slovakia a year after Hitler invaded, a yellow star sewn onto her baby carriage, Raine's childhood fear of being eaten by ravens, her grandmother's train trips to Vienna to visit Freud, people waxing the floor with candle ends and burying their silver in the garden, her five-year-old mother standing on street corners in Slovakia selling rats disguised as rabbits. There was something strangely convincing about her tales. Or could she be imagining it all?

"I sit there in biology wondering why the amphibians are disappearing," she said.

"What amphibians?" he said.

"They're vanishing—all over the world, even in remote places. I've read about it in the papers. Scientists think it's kind of ominous."

"I see here you have a psychiatrist," he said. "What does she think the trouble is?"

"With the amphibians?"

"With *you*."

"Dr. Hadcock says I'm suffering from some kind of extremism, an obsessive-compulsive disorder called scrupulosity. But she thinks someday I might be capable of acting like a normal person. Scrupulosity only occurs in Roman Catholics and Orthodox Jews. You want to know the definition? 'Habitual and unreasonable hesitation or doubt, coupled with anxiety, in connection with the making of moral judgments.' St. Ignatius Loyola had it, too."

"I've never heard of it," he said.

"My mental condition is one of the reasons I decided to come to St. Ursula's. To make my parents happy. They used to take me ice-skating at Rockefeller Center and watch me sprawled out on the ice in my jeans and puffy purple nylon jacket while some kid in tights and a skating skirt went speeding right past me and did a triple flip."

"So you think they're disappointed in you?" he asked. "Are you disappointed in yourself?"

"I know people think I *should* be, like there was something wrong with me because my hair was green and it wasn't St. Patrick's Day. But I think the human need to conform is not a trait that's lending itself to our survival. Not that I'm any great example of individuality now that I'm going around in this uniform that was once a happy sheep."

"Does wearing a uniform bother you? Does it disturb you to blend in? Not to be noticed?"

"I don't know," she said. "I do crave a fair amount of attention."

"What was your biggest problem at Horace Mann?"

"My fear and my laziness. I'm afraid of everything. I keep wondering if I'll get cancer. Maybe a nuclear bomb will kill me and my skin will peel off. Or I could inhale a speck of plutonium."

"I noticed reading through your records that you have some pretty unusual interests."

"Yeah," she said. "Like self-preservation."

The sun was rising over the steeple of St. Bartholomew's Church and shining onto the wet crab apples outside his window. "What do you do for fun?" he said.

"I spend time with my boyfriend, Pavel, hanging out in the garden—or in the summer, going to these Slovakian picnics. I play my bagpipes. I have a knife collection. I read comic books, the Torah, and biology books. One thing I learned is that animal survival depends on three things—what can kill them, what they can eat, and who they can mate with, in that order. The nuns say a kiss is the first step into the portals of hell, but Mary doesn't think so. She sleeps with the gardener anytime she feels like it, and she doesn't seem to mind when Pavel and I go up to my bedroom to celebrate the Jewish holidays. One night when Pavel's playing the *Romance de los Pinos* on his cello, I was thinking of climbing up to his room on a ladder, like George Sand did with Chopin."

Al was relieved that it was almost time for her to go. "And what do you plan to say to Pavel when he looks up and sees you climbing through his window?" he said.

She smiled. "I'll say, 'My heart is never an embarrassment to me.'"

He leaned forward. "Raine, I'm afraid you're going to have to commit yourself to making some changes. Soon. *Very* soon."

"Everything's always changing," she said. "Cherries become birds, fish become seagulls, grass becomes milk. But I want everything to stay the same. I want to be able to count on something. Then I keep wondering if the insects will go blind from the ultraviolet rays coming through the holes in the ozone layer and not be able to pollinate the plants. Don't you worry about that kind of stuff for your kids?"

"I don't have any kids," he said. "My wife wants them, but I never have."

"What do you want if you don't want kids?"

"I don't know. Peace and quiet, I guess."

"You'll have a lot of peace and quiet after we get clobbered with a Tomahawk cruise missile," she said.

* *

Raine got up early, did two push-ups, took a bath, washed her hair, put on her uniform, and stood gazing at herself in the mirror. A rather interesting creature gazed back at her, wearing a blue-and-green plaid jumper, a crisp white blouse, white socks, and brown loafers. The leaves on the tree in the garden were yellowing. It was her thirteenth day at St. Ursula's Academy.

She put on her sunglasses and felt like a character in a movie. "Celebrities live for themselves," she said to the image in the mirror. "Heroines live to redeem society."

When Mary asked her if she wanted the usual for breakfast—soy hot dogs with sauerkraut and grits—Raine said, "I'll have what normal people eat."

As she ate Mary's scrambled eggs and listened to the scraping sound of her knife spreading strawberry jam on toast, she pretended she was balancing a cup on her head. The scent of Persian violets drifted in from the garden. Fog was rising up out of the chrysanthemums. A bird was chirping. She was pleased with the calm and orderly turn her life had taken. Everything in her new life would be different. Colleges would offer her scholarships, but she would have to decline, explaining that she had been called to rescue the world from its collective stupidity. Student reporters would arrive to interview her. *The daring exploits of the girl with the X-ray eyes astonishes nuns who have never seen anything like her!*

All along the walk down Riverside Drive, up the steps and through the heavy doors of St. Ursula's Academy, Raine thought of her stellar academic future, but in class, she caught herself lapsing into one of her Pavel reveries. At the end of the day, when she put on her backpack and went to buy herself some bubble gum ice cream at Mr. Wizlutsky's candy store, she felt she had deteriorated into her old self. She hated seeing the homeless people on Broadway, lying in alcoves beside their fat plastic bags of belongings, or scavenging through the garbage for refundable bottles. When she heard a woman in a ripped coat coughing, she was sure the woman had cancer, and by the time she turned onto West 88th Street and walked up the steps of her house, she was feeling sick herself.

She changed her clothes and went back outside, her pockets full of Mary's chocolate-chip cookies, and sat on a bench on Broadway, hoping someone she knew would come along. But no one did. She wondered if the man sitting beside her was a Nazi. He was probably too young, but he may have been the son of a Nazi. She doubted that guilt could be passed down from father to son. That meant there was always the possibility of a new world—the chance to begin again with innocence, with new flesh.

She stopped into the American Museum of Natural History and went straight to the hall of masks. She loved the curly beards of the old rain gods, the Aztec skull mask inlaid with turquoise, the red earth masks mixed with coconut oil and trimmed with shells, feathers, and bark. She read a placard on the wall, which said: *The mask is endowed with power by the interaction of the artist, the wearer, and the spectator. A mask usually covers the face and conceals the identity as well as the personality and mood of the wearer. With its own features, it establishes another being. Primitive man used the mask for many reasons: to assure a plentiful harvest or a productive hunt; to ward off evil; to celebrate rites initiating boys into manhood; to visualize either the unknown or the well known. A mask is a form of disguise that connects the wearer with spiritual powers, thereby acting as a protection against mysterious and alien forces in the universe.*

After she left the museum, she walked across Central Park through Dr. Hadcock's neighborhood, wondering what Dr. Hadcock said about her patients to her husband, Harold. She sat down on a bench overlooking the East River and wrote in her journal:

"I have this young patient who's crazy."

"I thought all your patients were crazy," Harold says, refilling her martini glass.

"This girl cannot accept the world as it is, and that's what a crazy person is. She thinks some Slovakian boy is in love with her. I believe he is a complete figment of her imagination."

"Well, if anyone can help her, you can."

"It's her parents who need help. Her mother is a concert violinist, her father is an astronomer, and they were leading this idyllic life until the mother got pregnant when she was forty-one. [Trumpets and bagpipes begin to play in the background.] They both had fabulous careers. They live in a five-bedroom townhouse. They have a garden. They have a Porsche."

"Was the girl born crazy?"

"She was completely normal until she had a bat mitzvah ceremony, but her parents didn't show up for it, and after that, the world started to drive her mad."

"So what are you going to do with her, Cheryl?"

"I plan to recommend electroshock therapy and six months in the Rikers Island Psychiatric Hospital for the Partially Insane. But her future looks dubious since she has this rare disease called scrupulosity, which will rob her life of fun and joy."

"Thank goodness our children are perfect," Harold replies.

Raine turned to the white-haired couple sitting next to her on the bench and said, "I just started at this new school. St. Ursula's Academy. It's on 79th and Riverside." They were looking at her quizzically. The man had translucent white pouches under his eyes. The woman was wearing a navy blue dress with pineapples on it. It reminded Raine of a dress her grandmother had worn. "I've been there since the end of August, and I'm trying to fit in, but I'm just beginning to realize that I'm afraid of kids my age. You know why? Because teenagers, myself included, are very judgmental. I believe people become judgmental because they're insecure. At my other school, I hung out with the punks and it was okay because we all looked alike and acted alike and we didn't judge each other but we judged everyone else. We thought people were intolerant. We thought we were nonconformists, but we were really just another clique. I am basically a very idealistic and slothful person. I seem friendly because I talk to strangers, but at school I am very, very quiet around other kids. I hate going through the cafeteria line and not knowing who I can sit with, so usually I skip lunch and hang out in the yard with the St. Ursula's statue. It's very indicative of me that I have absolutely no trouble talking to a piece of cement, but I cannot think of one thing to say to people between the ages of thirteen and nineteen. I'm capable of worshipping some of them, but I can't really relate to any of them, except occasionally to this boy I know. He's my boyfriend, but I'm not his girlfriend, and the yin and yang are really out of whack because of it. My best friend, Mary, lived with an alcoholic for twelve years, until she came to live with my parents. I was a one-year-old who screamed all the time, but I guess living with a shrieking baby is better than living with a husband who drinks. I plan to take care of Mary when she gets old. I don't care what's wrong with her—she's definitely not going to a nursing home." The man was gazing at the lamppost. The woman was doing a crossword puzzle. "It's a pretty strange world, in my opinion," she continued. "Zap the bugs, drop the bombs, go directly to death, do not pass Go, do not collect two hundred dollars. I'm thinking of starting this group. St. Ursula's Girls Against the Atomic Bomb."

The man turned to her and smiled. His eyes—a dull, smoky brown—began to sparkle. "Tell her," he said to the woman.

"Tell her what?" she said.

"I worked on the atom bomb," he said. "I watched it explode. I could feel the wind in my pants. It was brighter than the sun. It turned the clouds to ice. When I was in the hospital for my angina trouble last month, this doctor came in, all dressed up in this fifteen-hundred-dollar Madison Avenue suit, and she said, 'You're one of them.' She kept saying that. 'You're one of them.' Off the charts on the

Geiger counter."

"That's absolutely horrible," Raine said.

"She told me I could get leukemia. I was in the Army, stationed in Nevada. 1952. I'm seventy-one now. Well, you can't live forever. If I was the President, I'd drop the thing. That's what it was made for. I wouldn't want to be there, though."

"No one would," Raine said. "That's the point."

"I'd drop it on the bastards. Then you'd show them what it was made for. Right?" He seemed to be growing younger and happier as he spoke. "St. Ursula's Girls Against the Atomic Bomb? That's good. The son always protests what the father has done. I wish you luck."

"I wish you luck, too," she said, getting up. "Both of you. May the road rise to meet you."

Raine walked over to Second Avenue and went into her favorite thrift shop. She loved the womanly scent in the limp clothes, and she liked to imagine the lives of the women who had owned the clothes, the moods they were in when they wore them, the words that had been said to them, and the words they wished had been said.

"I used to be more of a shopper," she said to Iris, who owned the store. "But I wear a uniform now. It's a plaid jumper, but I'm working my way up to stripes with a number on it."

Iris was standing under a flickering fluorescent light,

her orange hair tied in a ponytail over one ear. Raine could see she had been using her freckle-removing cream again. "How's the new school, Raine?" she said.

"I've been there over two weeks, but I haven't made any friends."

"Well, just try, dear. That's all you can do."

"It's very hard being in love and trying to please your parents at the same time."

"Who's the lucky boy?"

"His name is Pavel Orzagh."

"Bring him in," Iris said. "I'd like to meet him."

"Pavel brings me places. He doesn't get brought anywhere. I have his picture. Want to see it?" She handed Iris the photograph and said, "We play the bagpipes together. In Slovakian, it's called the *gajdy*."

"Well, watch out for the kind of music you make, dear. Before you know it, you could be listening to lullabies."

Raine was looking through a box of lace bras and wondering if breasts were meant to be propped up or if bras were some kind of unnecessary constriction like hoop skirts and whalebone corsets. Her mother told her that before she was born, some women burned their bras at a Miss America pageant, but her mother always wore a bra herself. Mary did not wear a bra, or high heels, or lipstick. Men and girls wore uniforms, whereas women got to pick what they wanted to look like. But your personality came with you. It was like a package deal to Florida—kind of chintzy but you were supposed to see what you could do with it—grow and change and turn yourself into someone quite marvelous. It was all up to her.

She held up a dress covered with red sequins. Pavel would consider it trashy. "Do you think this dress will make me look like Jello Biafra?" she asked Iris.

"Wouldn't it be better just to look like yourself?"

"Hitler wore this greasy bowler hat with a caftan like the ones Hasidic Jews wore. Don't you think that's ironic? My grandmother met him in Vienna when he was toasting prints in the oven and selling them on street corners as the work of the Old Masters."

"Really?" Iris said, sounding very uninterested.

Raine walked home up Third, across 40th, up Lexington, across 50th, up Park, across 60th, up Madison, across 70th, up Fifth and across the park. She tried to walk calmly and evenly, sensing that her new life as a St. Ursula's girl had become sacrosanct and could be easily disturbed, thrown off its axis, and Pavel thrown off with it.

* *

"I have a new student," Al said to Frieda as he looked out the kitchen window. "That girl across the way. See her? She's in her garden, doing a headstand."

Frieda got up and looked out the window. "The Rassaby girl?"

"You know her?"

"No—but I've talked to her father in church. He works at the planetarium."

"I'm worried about her," Al said.

Frieda laughed. "You always worry about your students. And how far does it get you or them?"

"I can't help it," he said. "You worry about your patients, too."

"You've always taken St. Ursula's home with you, Al. I try to leave my concern about my patients at work."

"But emotions aren't something you can turn on and off, are they?"

"It isn't about emotions," Frieda said. "It's about respecting the boundaries around your work and your life."

He made their coffee as slowly as possible. He could feel her receding as she sat at the kitchen table, reading the newspaper. He sensed a tightness in her that he hadn't noticed before, something about to snap.

"You're putting sugar into the coffeepot, Alvin."

"Sorry," he said. He turned to her, unable to think of an appropriate opening, and said, "It bothers me that that social worker at the nursing home goes into the sewers to feed homeless people. You won't go down there with him, will you?"

"Of course not."

"It could be dangerous," he said.

"Feeding the homeless is something Daniel does in his free time."

Al wondered if the street people liked this young man dropping down into their gloomy tunnels with his bag of sandwiches. Hadn't they gone underground for their own reasons that may have had something to do with *privacy*?

"I love that about Daniel," Frieda added.

"You love what?"

"That he's compassionate. And open to exploration."

For Al, being open to exploration would mean looking deeply into Frieda's eyes—*really* looking and finding the courage to see what she had hidden there.

"All married people are like this," he said, turning back to the chrome coffeepot in which he could see a sort of fun-house reflection of himself with huge ears and dark, hungry eyes.

"Like what?" she said.

His back was to her. "We had a very short engagement. Not much time to deliberate. I swept you off your feet."

She laughed and said, "No you didn't."

"You didn't know what hit you. Remember how I used to sing under your window?"

"The neighbors hated you."

"It was love singing."

"It was very sweet," she said.

"Love doesn't sing anymore."

She came up behind him and slipped her arms around his waist. "Oh Alvin! You're such a worrier," she said. "When birds sing, it's out of fear, or because they're looking for a mate. Married people don't have to sing because the mating game is over."

He turned around to her. "The mating game is over?"

"Of course it is, and it *is* a game. A biological one. You were trying to woo me so you had to sing to impress me. Now you don't have to do that anymore."

"You mean I'm just imagining it?" he said.

"Imagining what?"

That you're tired of me, he wanted to say, but what came out was, "That I drink too much."

"You probably do drink too much," she said. "Maybe you should take a look at that."

"At what?"

"At the reason you have to anesthetize yourself every night."

She returned to the table and leafed through the newspaper as he stood listening to the liquid gurgling through the coffeepot.

Their bedroom during the last year, with its gray walls and prim white molding, had become a refuge from sex. Al feared that making love would result in procreation, while Frieda feared it would not. He was secretly and guiltily afraid she would trick him, becoming pregnant without his consent—so bed for them now was mostly associated with reading and sleep.

Children had never been an issue until Frieda's thirty-fifth birthday three years ago. He had taken her to an Indian restaurant overlooking Central Park, and after her second pot of jasmine tea, she said, "Would you like to have a baby?" His instant response was, "No." The question seemed to him like a kind of betrayal. Wasn't she happy with him? Wasn't he enough for her? Was she getting bored with him? Whenever the subject came up, he tried to evade it. Several uncomfortable talks had followed. Now they no longer discussed having children.

He hated the idea of a child coming into the world with a parent as unwilling as he was. He imagined Frieda and the child forming an alliance, growing closer and closer as Al grew more distant and detached. During his boyhood, he remembered taking the train up to the farm with his grandmother and looking for men who resembled him and therefore might possibly be his father. Occasionally he found one, and he stared at him for a long time and finally could not resist telling his grandmother. But she never even turned to look at the man.

He poured their coffee, imagining honesty and truth welling up between him and Frieda—his thoughts and her thoughts becoming *their* thoughts. But the setting wasn't right. The kitchen was too staid and ordinary a cage for the nightingale to sing in.

* *

Raine loved the nights she slept in Mary's bed, curled up into her warm, round body, her face pressed into Mary's black hair, the smell of dried heather in her sheets, years and years in her bed before Mary put her out when she was thirteen. "You're a woman now," Mary announced. "Woman does not sleep with woman. Woman sleeps with man."

"With man?" Raine said.

"Now you must take on the responsibilities of a woman and know that a woman who is wise does not tell her stories all at once."

When Raine was a baby, Mary carried her on her back all day, and while she cooked, cleaned, and watered the garden, Raine could hear her mother practicing the violin. She remembered the feel of Mary's plump, warm shoulders, her shiny black hair, the smell of chocolate pudding bubbling on the stove, the beautiful wailing of her mother's violin. After spending two years on Mary's back, she began to look closely at the world and see that there were spectacular currents under life—fantastic possibilities and unseen things.

She loved the white walls of Mary's room hung with lisle curtains and her collection of whalebones, soapstone, and rose quartz. She loved the cotton dresses hanging in a row in the open closet, and all the knitted blankets and shawls and beads Mary kept but never wore in the top drawer of her bureau, beside her necklace of polar bear teeth.

As a child, Raine sat in the bluish, wavering lamplight of Mary's room off the kitchen, hearing about the seasons of starvation and plenty in northern Greenland. As she spoke, Mary would croak like a raven or bark like a fox. Her stories always ended with, "This too is a story. This is how its words go."

When Raine's parents were home, Mary did not sit in the dining room and eat with them, but when Karel and Raisa were away, Raine and Mary ate together in the kitchen. Raine would sometimes try to get Mary to laugh and some nights they laughed so hard, they couldn't eat. She loved having Mary all to herself.

Mary had explained to her that people in any land do what their people expect of them because human beings are not solitary like polar bears, wandering over the ice, looking for seals, but are tied to other creatures. The world, she said, is governed by Sila, Taqqiq, Siqiniq, and Kannaaluk—time, the moon, the sun, and the girl at the bottom of the sea. Before the great animals of the land and sea appeared and ended the primordial confusion, life was without danger but also without the joy that comes with effort and exertion.

In the place Mary came from, a land of polished black marble, yellow poppies, and red saxifrage, sometimes it was seventy degrees below zero, the sun either never came up or never went down, and ten people full of lice lived together all winter in a three-room snow house. If there were no ducks or caribou or walrus left in the caves under the snow, people did not eat. Human beings have no feeling of living, Mary said, when there are no difficulties to surmount.

Summer or winter, Mary sat in the garden every morning, then worked all day shopping, cooking, and cleaning the house. At four o'clock, she started preparing dinner. She washed the dishes and scoured the kitchen. She rarely got angry at Raine, but when she did, she said, "You wear pants of dogskin!" When Mary cooked soup, she split the marrowbone and took out the slippery marrow and ate it, like a long, fat worm.

As a child, Raine was constantly afraid that Mary would die, and she pictured Mary's kinfolk arriving, chattering in Greenlandic and going off with her body, hoisting it onto a dogsled parked outside the door. She imagined waking up after Mary had gone, hearing the faint sound of sleigh bells and feeling a great emptiness falling over the house.

* *

"I hope you like my nail polish," Raine said, plopping down in the chair in Al's office and holding out her hands. Al winced. Her nails were painted black and each one was covered with a tiny decal of a yellow star of David.

"Very creative," he said.

"You're the only one who listens to me, Mr. K. Mary's always been a good listener, but she's getting bored with my tales of woe."

"What about your parents. Don't they listen?"

"Daddy listens when he takes me out to lunch—but that's only because he wants something."

"What does he want?"

"He wants me to be little again."

"What about your mom?" he said.

"She takes me on these shopping trips to Bloomingdale's and buys me these really shmendrick clothes, and I end up trying on the stuff she picks for me, quite reluctantly, believe me, because my mother does not understand the word NO. She stands there in the dressing room, and she beams and says, 'It's adorable!' and it probably *is* adorable, but I try to tell her that that is not the look I'm striving for. So she turns to the saleswoman and says, 'We'll take it.' Then we go over to the Plaza for tea, and I have to wear my new purchase, and I am absolutely mortified thwamping down 59th Street looking like Queen Josephine fresh from the Baltics. Even the horses we pass take one look, roll their eyes, and think, 'Jesus, Mary, and Joseph, who dressed her?' Then we settle ourselves at her favorite table in the Palm Court, which is directly across from a mirror, and the waiter brings tea, I talk, and Mother keeps saying, 'Don't say that, dear.' Of course, she only calls me dear at the Plaza. At home, she calls me Raine Marie in this cold voice that could freeze an orangutan sitting on the equator. That's what I mean about you, Mr. K. You listen to me, and it feels like I've been blind my whole life and I can suddenly see a cherry tree."

He sat up a bit taller in his chair and said, "Thank you, Raine."

"My mother and I go shopping four times a year. We started when I was eight. That's forty trips to Bloomingdale's and forty trips to the Plaza. No wonder I'm seeing a psychiatrist."

"I'm sure Dr. Hadcock listens to you."

"She does. But she only listens if my parents pay her a hundred and thirty dollars an hour. Dr. Hadcock claims I'm interesting, but sometimes I find myself quite boring, and it's disturbing to think that Pavel might find me boring, too."

"You're not on earth to amuse Pavel."

"No, that's right—God fished me out of the vlei for some other mysterious reason. *Schwer zu sein ein Yid.*"

"What does that mean?" he said.

"It's hard to be a Jew."

He watched her in the hall after school, packing up her books and walking alone out of the building. Didn't the other girls talk to her? Didn't she talk with them? Did she want to see herself as an outsider? He wished he could arrange for her to be less lost in herself, to have friends, to be happy.

* *

Raine was sixteen when her grandmother started taking her to the Slovakian picnics in Harriman State Park. A five-piece band played music all afternoon and the picnic tables were covered with kale patties, fish pudding, red cabbage with caraway seeds, macaroni stuffing, boiled pork, salt rolls, blue carp, liver dumplings, cookies, jam-filled balls, and chestnut cake. Her grandmother danced to the fiddles and zithers while Raine wandered around listening to people telling stories about Slovakia—the blue Danube, the bacon grease sandwiches, the flax fields, the Hlinka Guard, the feel of dresses made of flour sacks. At the picnics, everyone laughed and ate and danced and shed tears over the day in 1939 when the Nazis arrived in Slovakia.

It was at one of the picnics that she had met Pavel Orzagh. He had olive skin, a thin face, big greenish eyes that turned gray when it rained, and silky brown hair filled with glints of gold. In his pockets, he carried a magnifying glass, a compass, a knife, and a jar of juniper oil mixed with lard that he kept in case he found a wounded bird. Pavel was always talking to the old people at the picnics, telling them jokes, or playing his *gajdy* and singing or dancing with the old women. He was fascinated by the Holocaust, but he wasn't obsessed by it. Raine took the doom much more personally, feeling threatened by humanity's cruel streak. She made lists of all the abominable things human beings had done throughout history, and pasted them in a scrapbook called *Horrible but True Things You'd Rather Not Know*.

Everything Pavel told her about Slovakia during the war left a searing impression upon her. Especially about the town crier appearing on the street corner and drumming in furious rhythm, then tucking his drumsticks into his drumstrap and rolling out a scroll announcing the newest racial laws. *The Jews must wear a yellow armband. The Jews must be in their homes except between 10 a.m. and 3 p.m. The Jews must wear a yellow star of David, which must be displayed even on baby carriages and cribs. The Jewish star must be affixed to every letter sent by a Jew.*

Sometimes Raine and Pavel lay on the grass and read to each other from *An Album of Nazism*. It said that Hitler read children's books, didn't eat meat, and rarely changed his mind. He loved to ride in fast cars and hated to go to bed. Three hundred Jews in Stuttgart were forced to lick the street while people stood around, laughing. "'A generation was being trained to accept atrocities without objection, to follow the state no matter where it led,'" Pavel read to her one Sunday. "'The survivors of the Holocaust are spread out across the world—from Israel to Illinois. Even their children are affected. Though born in freedom, the children of these victims often exhibit severe personal problems.'" He leaned over and touched her arm. "They're talking about *you*, Raine," he said.

A book of photographs Pavel had brought with him contained pictures of French children being sent to concentration camps—wearing hair ribbons, coats with velvet collars, polished shoes, and white socks folded carefully over the ankle. "Abel Herzberg says that it wasn't that six million Jews were killed," Pavel said, "but one Jew was killed, and then another and another, six million times." He was always quoting men with names like Bal Shem Tov, Salomon Benhamu, and Efraim Zuroff, and Raine always pretended she knew who they were.

On Sunday nights, after the picnics, the atmosphere of Slovakia began to bloom in her head—the ravens, the plum trees, the silver hidden in gardens, the vats of sauerkraut in the cellar, the white goose being fattened in a back room. Some days after school, she went down to the Lower East Side to spend time with the Hasidic Jews. She wondered what it was like to live openly and proudly as a Jew. Pavel and his mother were proud to be Jewish, and she loved their orthodoxy, their defiance, their reverence for the religion. The Holocaust had scared them—it scared everyone—but it did not make them hide from their past.

One Sunday afternoon, Raine and Pavel went into a cave, and before long, they were lying in each other's arms. She felt very grown-up to be lying on the ground together like a couple in the movies. She sighed and wished the war were still going on so they could travel across the ocean and work together in a dark room, printing false identification papers for the Jews. She closed her eyes and touched his back and pictured the beauty of his bones, smooth and white and hard like the moon. His lips tasted like juniper berries. His fingers unbuttoned her plaid blouse, and she felt his hands moving softly over her breasts, and she could tell he was exploring, he was lost, he was happy. When they sat up and leaned against the rocks covered with yellow lichen, Pavel said, "Lichen is the manna from heaven in the Old Testament."

"My grandmother used to walk with Sigmund Freud through the gardens of the Belvedere Palace," she said. "They walked the Ringstrasse and stopped in a café for coffee and marzipan."

"Cool," Pavel said.

"It wasn't really," she said. "A lot of people in Vienna hated Jews. The anti-Semites wore white carnations in their lapels." She imagined that her grandmother, walking beside Freud in Vienna, felt as she did, walking through the woods with Pavel.

Pavel collected mushrooms—rubbery tree ears, hard, burnt-looking birch mushrooms, purple oyster mushrooms, stone fungus with scattered scales, fan-shaped turkey tails, apricot- and cream-colored chanterelles. With a willow branch, he fished in the river and caught brown trout, their silver and violet scales wriggling in the sun. Sometimes at the picnics, he'd make a fire and cook the trout, but Raine refused to eat fish and hated the sound of trout bones crunching in Pavel's teeth.

She followed him into the woods, and they looked for truffles or owls and porcupines in the trees, or quail eggs, or mushrooms he would sell to the Vietnamese grocery. She liked the way he went from being boyish and careless and playful to being a man who held her in his arms. Other kids would sometimes join them, but Pavel was always the leader.

In the cornfields bordering the park, inside the deep green seams of corn, they played hide-and-seek. One Sunday, they swam together under the water lilies, circling each other, and then Raine came up behind him, and held onto him until they sank, and they popped up out of the water, laughing. Dragonflies glided by, the delicate legs of skatebugs skimmed the surface of the pond. Pavel plunged underwater and darted away, and she thought of the earth when it was new— the steaming creeks, the mats of blue-greens, the boiling pools of turquoise algae.

They got out of the water, sat on the bank, and listened to the band on the other side of the park playing Slovakian bandit songs, shepherd songs, or harvest songs. The world seemed dazzling on those Sundays, filled with unexplainable, unseen things.

Water lilies were floating on the pond. Pavel showed

her a beaver pond and told her that beavers loved felling aspen trees. "The problem is, they're too dumb to figure out which way the tree will fall," he said. They were squatting at the edge of the blue water when he said, "I like being with you."

"You do?"

"It feels nice."

"It does?"

"Don't you think so?"

She smiled. "It feels wonderful," she said.

They sat together for a long time, then Raine reached over, put her arms around him, and they rolled onto the ground, wrestling and laughing. Then he was still, and she felt his arms around her and the feel of his soft shirt against her skin.

He drew her bare feet into his lap and peeled the dried purple swamp mud from her toes. He did this with great concentration, and she closed her eyes, feeling the sun and his warm fingers on her skin. She smelled the sweet pepperbush in the swamp, which meant the end of summer.

"When I'm playing my cello, it's like meeting with God in the way the old rabbis talked about it, the place where there's only harmony and there's no beginning or middle or end. All I have to do is get out my cello, and I'm there. I want you to know everything about me because that's what love is, isn't it? Not hiding?"

"You are hiding," she said. "You're only saying what's good about you."

He laughed, and they got up and walked back to the picnic area. He sat across the table from her, eating cookie sticks with yolk icing as someone played Czech folksongs on an accordion.

They stood by the jasmine hedge, smiled at each other, and said goodbye as the band played Chopin's Revolutionary Etude—which had been broadcast on the radio for twenty-four hours the day Hitler marched into Poland.

* *

"When I was twelve, the missionaries came to Greenland," Mary said as she served asparagus quiche to Raine and her parents in the dining room. "They changed my name from Seewagak to Mary because they couldn't pronounce our names. They put up plastic crucifixes in the classroom. After that, I didn't want to go to school anymore, but when I told my old grandmother, she said, 'Go to school. Keep your eyes half-closed.'"

"Please, Mary," Raisa said. "Raine needs to keep her eyes open."

Mary laughed and said, "I was glad I followed grandmother's advice, because I did go back to school and I married the schoolteacher, and he brought me to New York, and I met all of you after I discovered he was a—"

"Mary, please," Raisa said. "We've heard this before,

and we do not want Raine falling in love with any school-teachers."

"I probably won't since they're all nuns," Raine said. "Besides, I already am in love."

"With that Slovakian gardener?" her father said.

"Pavel's working at the Bronx Botanical Garden to save money for college. He's a Jew who's proud of being a Jew, unlike us—and that is something I find very seductive."

"Raine, we are *not* Jews," Raisa said as Mary slipped back into the kitchen. "Your father is Catholic, as you well know, and my mother converted to Judaism *after* she emigrated from Slovakia. That's when she started all that nonsense with the dishes and the holidays. She was always doing something bizarre when I was a child like making me send out *shanah tovah* cards."

"She was kind enough to read me the Book of Lamentations on the Ninth Day of Av," Raine said. "And on Purim, Vikey got so drunk she couldn't tell the difference between 'Blessed be Mordechai' and 'Cursed be Haman.'"

"Raine, *please*," Raisa said.

"St. Paul said that Adam made sin a part of human nature, but the rabbis always thought the human was a wondrous and harmonious being. That's really why I chose to become a Jew."

"Let's ask Mary to bring in some ice cream for the pie," Raisa said, ringing the little silver bell she kept beside her wine glass. Raisa's hair was sparkling and Raine thought of how it must have felt to be the kind of child the Nazis wanted—a blonde, blue-eyed beauty dressed in a potato sack dress. What if Raisa had been exported to Germany to strengthen the Aryan race?

Mary appeared in the doorway, smiling.

"Do we have any ice cream?" Raisa said.

"Strawberry," Mary said.

"Strawberry always reminds me of those awful birthday parties we used to have for Raine, when practically no one showed up and everyone's heart was broken," Raisa said.

"I can run down to Mr. Wizlutsky's and get some other kind," Mary said.

"Oh no—don't bother," Karel said.

"If you wouldn't mind, Mary," Raisa said.

"It won't take me any time," Mary said, and Raine pictured Mary trotting down to Broadway and back with her straight hair bouncing on her shoulders, and when she returned, collapsing into a chair and having a heart attack.

"I'll go," Raine said.

"Vanilla, please," Raisa said to Mary.

The door swung closed, and Karel said to Raine, "So what can you tell us about school?"

"The Mother Superior and the guidance counselor have been really nice to me."

"Good," Raisa said.

"See that window over there with the ivy hanging down? That's where my guidance counselor, Mr. Klepatar, lives."

"We should make an appointment to meet him," Raisa said. "Maybe we've left too much up to Mary."

"I don't know where we'd be without Mary," Karel said. "Remember what life was like before we hired her?"

Raisa laughed. "Raine either had to be moving or listening to my violin. It was the only thing that calmed her down."

"It was awful," Karel said. "Mary saved us."

"After Raine graduates, Mary's going back to Greenland," Raisa said.

"What do you mean?" Raine said. "Mary is *not* going back to Greenland. She's a New Yorker. She loves life on the fast track."

"Mary is steeped in Eskimo ideas," Raisa said.

"And what about your plans?" Karel said. "You'll be graduating in June. Then what?"

"What do you mean?"

"Have you given any thought to college?"

"College?" Raine said.

"Yes," Karel said.

"Vikey never went to college, and she was a heroine. Don't you think so?"

They were silent until Mary returned and served the ice cream, which was a pale creamy green, glistening in the candlelight with chunks of chocolate. Mary maintained her independence in the household by never doing exactly as she was told.

"Thank you, Mary," Raisa said. "You can go to your room. Raine will be doing the dishes tonight."

"Good night then," Mary said.

"Good night, Mary," Raine said. She looked at her mother. "You don't think Vikey was a heroine?"

"Of course I do," Raisa said, her eyes meeting Raine's. "My mother was an extraordinary woman. But children of extraordinary people usually have a steep price to pay."

"But what price have you paid? You're alive, aren't you? You mean you wish she didn't hide those Jews in her cellar?"

"I'm not saying that," Raisa said. "But do you have any idea what would have happened to us if she had been caught?"

"Heroic people always threaten everybody," Raine said. "When Galileo used the telescope, it was a radical departure from accepted thought, right Daddy?"

"You're not living in the real world," Raisa said.

"I am living in the real world, Mother. I'm living right at the edge of something. I'm like a bird who jumps out of its nest at midnight when the cat jumps in." Raine dished out seconds of ice cream for everyone and said, "I've been thinking about a lot of things lately and I realize that I dragged you two through hellacious times last year. It wasn't that I was trying to. It was more like I didn't really think about you and now I wish I had. I want you to know that I understand you've both sacrificed a lot for me, and I doubly appreciate it since I know you didn't want children."

"That's not true," Raisa said.

"Raine, of course we wanted you," Karel said. "And you know what, dear? We love you exactly the way you are."

"You do? Since when?" she said, and they laughed.

* *

Vikey was born in Banska Stiavnica, Slovakia, in 1903, and she died in 1997, when Raine was seventeen. It was a good time to be born, she said, because to live is a privilege, even if the Nazis decided to march into your homeland and kill two of your cousins and your sisters, Gitta and Sessi. Still, the world was beautiful, she said—full of astonishing things.

If a Slovakian swore an oath after putting a clod of earth on his or her head, or swallowing it, the oath became binding and incontestable, Vikey said. Sometimes Raine heard her whisper, "Mother, I come from you, you carry me, you nourish me, and you will take me after my death." Then she swallowed some dirt from the potted geranium on the windowsill. For many years, on Mary's day off, Vikey took care of Raine, sitting her down at the kitchen table in her apartment, putting on a white starched apron and cooking them dumplings or cabbage soup or hot *porkolt*, veal in a thick paprika gravy, or *bryndzove halusky*, noodles made of potatoes which she served with sheep's cheese.

Vikey had a lot of rules in her kitchen. She ate only fish with fins and scales and only mammals with cloven hooves and ruminating stomachs, and they had to be killed with a quick slash to the throat so that the blood ran out. She kept two separate dish rags to clean the counters, and she had dairy spatulas and meat spatulas, Passover dishes and everyday dishes and meat dishes, dishtowels trimmed with yellow to dry the plates after blintzes and dishtowels trimmed with red to dry the plates after meat. "You are not only washing dishes," Vikey said. "You are tending to something that is ancient."

As she worked in the kitchen, she told Raine the stories of Rachel, Dinah, Deborah, Rebecca, and Yokheved. "The Torah says, 'Now the sons of Jacob were twelve in number,' but his daughter, Dinah, was not mentioned," she said one day when Raine was twelve. "Shechem took her but did not respect her, and it was a matter not of animal instinct but of human aggression and appetite—of violence, not desire."

Raine watched Vikey paint the white of an egg onto the challah. They drank strong black Turkish coffee and ate pancakes with apricot jam. Vikey told her about their relatives in the photographs hanging on the walls. Her grandmother's shadowy past seemed enchanting, and Raine loved the Hasidic blessing Vikey taught her, *When you walk across the fields with your mind pure and holy, then from all the stones, and all growing things, and all animals, the sparks of their soul come out and cling to you, and then they are purified and become a holy fire in you.*

Vikey said that tulips were a sign of hope and she sometimes stopped at the fruit stand near her building to buy one tulip, which was all she could afford. "God sees if you believe or not—if you're full of hope, God sees." If God could see a flower in a vase on the table in Vikey's apartment, Raine wondered, how come he couldn't see Auschwitz or Bergen-Belsen? But it did no good to ask Vikey questions like that. She would only say that a fool can ask more questions in an hour than a wise woman could answer in seven years.

Raine loved it on Purim when she got to make as much noise as she wanted every time Vikey read the name of Haman. Vikey expected her to memorize prayers and to put half of her allowance into the *tsedakah* box, and when Raine told her about Pavel, she said, "The world turns and times change, but man and woman are always the same. There is no time and no season in a cave, so it is a comforting place. Boys overcome their fears by going into caves."

Raine loved hearing about the storks, synagogues, and clock towers in Banska Stiavnica, the blue Danube slinking through meadows of white poppies, and the wild boars running through beech forests. She believed her grandmother when she told her that the very first birds on Earth, preserved in an ancient lime ooze, had fallen into a coral lagoon in Banska Stiavnica.

Vikey bought a live carp every year for Passover, killed it with a club, and pared off its scales with a huge knife to make gefilte fish. She always had to have the fattest, shiniest fish with the clearest eyes, so she bought the fish a week before Passover, brought it home in a bucket, and put it in the bathtub where Raine talked to it and fed it lettuce and breadcrumbs. When Raine got angry about Vikey killing the fish, Vikey said, "My grandmother had a shochet come every Friday to slaughter the chickens and a goose for Shabbat dinner. It is a habit handed down as habits are and then they become traditions, which are an anchor for our people."

When Raine told her about her fears, Vikey said, "Fear isn't something to be gotten rid of. It's something real and human, something to pay attention to. Drunks are fearless but that doesn't make them courageous. Fear is a signal, to be honored and listened to. It was proper for us to be afraid of the Nazis and the Hlinka Guard and not berate ourselves for our fears."

She poured two glasses of sweet plum brandy made by the man who lived upstairs and said, "The Jewish holidays always celebrated the stories of God's protection, but the Holocaust makes us think about God's silence."

"Why was God silent about such a horrible thing?" Raine said.

"You are full of questions, dear," she said. "But in our day, children did not ask questions."

Raine wished they could cry together about the Holocaust, but they couldn't, Vikey said, because the ancient Romans had taught humanity that grief speaks but great grief is dumb. Vikey told her that it would be her job to find new answers to old riddles and new riddles for the children of the future.

Raine believed her parents loved her, but her grandmother showed her what love felt like, and until you learned that, she doubted you could sort out true love from false love, no matter how old you were.

* *

"Eureka!" Raine shouted, jumping up from her chair in Al's office. "You like me!"

"Of course I like you," Al said, squirming in his seat.

"I mean, that's why when I walk in here I feel like the bulls running through Pamplona."

"I like all the students I work with," he said.

"But you couldn't like them all equally, right?"

"Wrong. It's my job to invest as much energy as I can in each of my students."

"In the Talmud, it says, 'Every blade of grass has an angel bending over it, whispering, *Grow, grow*.' I can tell you like me. Do you have any idea how many people don't? They compose a group you could barely fit into Yankee Stadium."

He laughed and said, "I'm sure that isn't true."

"How many friends do you think I have?" she said.

"You've already told me. One."

"And she's a fifty-three-year-old foreigner. My own people do not care for me. Mrs. Orzagh, a fellow Slovakian, considers me an abomination. I think she's trying to turn Pavel against me."

"If Pavel cares for you, it won't make any difference what his mother thinks."

"He loves me, but he won't admit it. How ersatz is that? He and his mother think of me as this phony Jew who's going to Catholic school and knows nothing whatsoever about the Diaspora, and to complicate everything, they consider my parents anti-Semitic. But it isn't that Karel and Raisa don't like Jews. It's that they don't like Slovakians."

"Raine, please—you're working yourself into a froth. Can you think a calming thought?"

"I can try. But there might be a mushroom cloud in it."

* *

Al heard someone yelling, and he raised the screen and poked his head out the window. Raine was standing in the dirt lot below his den. "Hey, Mr. K! I met this fantastic nun. I had to come tell you. Should I come up?"

"No," he said. "Please don't."

"You come down then."

He looked over at the novel he was reading about Lancelot, which lay open on the table. "I can't," he said. "I'm busy."

"Her name is Sister Claudette. She hates stealth bombers. She despises nuclear weapons. It's the best thing that's happened to me since I met Russell Schweickart when I was eleven. The astronaut who flew in the first lunar module? I loved him because he really thought about things, and he asked questions that were hard to answer. Even though I was homesick in Alabama, and I snuck out a lot to call Mary, I absolutely adored meeting him, and I've always felt that I'd see him again when I was an adult, and we'd fall madly in love. Pavel isn't exactly astronaut material, but he reminds me a little of Russell Schweickart."

"Everyone in the entire neighborhood can hear every word you're saying," Al said.

"I'm shouting so you can hear me."

"I'd better come down," he said. He hurried down the stairs, and they stood on the steps leading to the street. The railing was coated with rust. Tiny white flowers had sprung up through the cracks in the concrete.

"Sister Claudette grew up in New Orleans and was

raped by her uncle," Raine said. "She's not terribly fond of men. I told her that putting people in groups and using them as scapegoats is humanity's worst trait, but I like the fact that she's not perfect. I wouldn't be at all surprised if she was having sex with a priest. She's been arrested seven times."

"For what?"

"Once, she rode up the Thames River in Connecticut in a canoe and painted *NO* on the hull of the U.S.S. *Ohio*, which is five feet longer than the Washington Monument. She makes me look like little Miss Muffet sitting on her tuffet."

"You really don't need someone else to emulate, Raine. Stay away from her."

"I probably should. But meeting her was like Paul meeting God on the road to Damascus."

"You can slum around with radical nuns after you get your diploma, but for now, it's nose to the grindstone. Q.E.D."

"My father says that, too. It's Latin. It means, 'I am the cowboy, you are the horse.'"

"First graduate—then go to jail with Sister Claudette if you want."

"It was an amazing experience to talk to someone who is not apathetic."

"Pavel isn't apathetic," he said.

"No—but at times I become distracted by you-know-what."

"No, I don't know what, and I don't want to know what. When you talk to me, please don't say everything you think."

"Extroverts do not live in a gated community. We think it, then BAM—we say it."

Al sighed. "Where did you meet this nun?"

"On a bench in the East Village. There's something very homesick about bench people—like we're looking for something that other people have, but we don't know what it is. We're different from people who go straight home."

"You're a very unfocused young woman, and if you don't begin to focus, I'm fearful of what will happen to you."

"I wouldn't mind meeting Frieda," she said.

"She isn't home. She works the three-to-eleven shift at an old folks' home. She's a nurse."

"That's rather heroic. I'm hoping someday I'll do something equally noble with my life."

"Well, you better get busy," he said. "You're over here talking to me when you could be home, studying."

"My parents are away, and Mary never tells me to study. She thinks I'm her reincarnated grandfather, and she's very uncomfortable telling him what to do."

"Raine, I'm busy. Could we talk about this tomorrow?"

"Certainly. I should go, too. I'm having dinner at the Salvation Army with Sister Claudette. She's really excited about St. Ursula's Girls Against the Atomic Bomb. Do you think you could help me round up some students?"

"No."

"Could you please just talk it up, Mr. K? Since you're my school sponsor?"

"What do you mean?" he said.

"We have to have a sponsor for it to be an official school group. So I put your name on the form. I knew you wouldn't mind."

He took a deep breath and said, "What made you think so?"

"Because you're always so nice to me."

"Raine, I would be derelict in my duty if I encouraged your involvement in this silly, illusory bomb group."

"What's silly and illusory about it?" she said.

"We all have to make choices, and this nun may be the greatest person you've ever met, but you don't have time for her."

"I love being a Jew, but I kind of wish I was Catholic because Catholics feel so guilty. St. Ursula's will be a great place to begin my bomb group. I tried in my other school, but I swear those kids don't have consciences. I'm expecting my group to spread like the plague at St. Ursula's because Catholics feel guilty even when they're innocent."

"Raine, I can't earn a diploma for you. But I can't give

up on you either."

"Why can't you?" she said.

"Because I'm getting a salary to encourage you to succeed."

"But what is success, exactly?"

"Success?" he said. "It's getting out of St. Ursula's Academy with a cap on your head."

* *

Raisa's hair was swept up in a tortoiseshell clip. She was wearing a white silk dress and pearls. Karel had on his gray suit with a white shirt and red silk tie. The three of them were having breakfast at the Hotel Pierre.

"Oh my God, I had this awful dream!" Raine said.

"What was it about?" Raisa asked.

"Oh God—this big green mountain and on the other side of it, a great big red thing like a tree sticking up into the sky. It was fire, and the top of it kept opening and it looked alive and kept swelling and rising up higher and higher, and then it kept going even higher, up past the sky. First it was red, then it turned different colors, and then Pavel came running up the hill without his clothes and said, 'That plane crashed into the sun!'"

Raisa frowned. "Have your nightmares gotten any better since you've been seeing Dr. Hadcock?"

"I don't know," Raine said. "They're worse when I stay up late. I was up 'til one in the morning reading this civil

defense manual I found in the library called *Atomic Attack*.
It was published by the government in the fifties. Maybe
your parents read it to you as a kid, before you went to
sleep. You know what it said? 'Children should be taught to
fall instantly to the floor, face-down, elbows out, eyes shut.
Should practice falling every night before bedtime.'"

"You see why you have nightmares?" Raisa said.

"Sometimes I can feel my Hiroshima *Weltanschauung*
fading. That's like a tree with red camellias on it and the
cicadas chirping and the smell of tempura made out of
pine needles and maple leaves and air raid shelters full of
mosquitoes, guns going *pum-pum-pum* and bombs going
da-don! da-don! da-don! and a white flash when the cicadas
stop singing, the sun disappears, and a greasy rain starts to
fall. I've had it since I was little. Other girls dream of sug-
arplums, but in my mind I can see the grass turning to
purple glass."

When Raine got home, she flopped down on the floor
of her bedroom, took out her pen, and wrote:

> *Sister Claudette is really quite saintly. She blazes with
> inner light. She usually wears jeans and a leather jacket,
> with a gold cross around her neck. When she looks at me, I
> feel like I'm underwater being stared at by a blue-eyed
> scallop. All her years in prison have both calmed down and
> fired up her moral fervor, and her determination is evident to
> all who stand beside her. I've always pictured myself incar-*

cerated—not in a prison but in a mental hospital with locked wards and bubble gum-pink walls, wearing a housedress and oxfords with ankle socks. She said her first night in jail they put her in solitary, and she pounded her fists on the mattress and said, "I'm not a resister—I'm not a resister!" She says the most dazzling things, like, "We can't build a new world without dismantling the dangerous old world first," and "Conspiracy means breathing together." I shared these quotes with Mother, and she said, "What does that mean?" I was furious. "Sister Claudette speaks English—do I have to translate her for you?" I said. Then I immediately had to wrap a towel around my head and envision myself sitting under the banyan tree like the Buddha or I would have said something terrible, Mother would have looked like a homeless kitten, I would have apologized ten thousand times, she would have glided up the stairs for a nap, and I would have flomped into the hammock to deliberate on my inability to get along with Homo sapiens.

After these exchanges with Mother, I sometimes have a picnic with the Seven Deadly Sins. I sit on a plaid blanket in the park and have a discussion with one of them—Pride, Covetousness, Lust, Anger, Gluttony, Envy, or Sloth. I usually eat some cabbage strudel from Tuszynska's and at my Gluttony Picnic I eat stale bread and wine. Gluttony is one of my worst sins, because I'm always looking for more, but anger, which seems to me like a good trait, really is my favorite deadly sin. At my Anger Picnics, I take my backpack and bat it on the ground like a lunatic, and I can feel the venom creeping out of me like a bee who has just stung someone. After a couple of Anger Picnics, I decided that I'm proud of my anger—it's my sword and I'm not planning to give it up. Tolerance allowed two-thirds of the Jews in Eastern Europe to be killed. Sometimes I wear a button saying, The Truth Will Set You Free, but First It Will Make You Mad. At my Sloth Picnic, I watch the ants hauling off the crumbs from my lunch and vow to spend less time sitting on the benches on Broadway, lying in the hammock, roaming around music stores, and plopped in the dogwood tree. Concerning my Covetousness and Envy Picnic, there's an extreme pecking order at St. Ursula's, so I never actually talk to Christy O'Kusky, but I spend mucho grandiose time eavesdropping while she stands in the halls at school, and everybody stands around her, listening to her say cool things.

Christy's the President of T.Au.M., which is Latin for Be Silent or Die, and I think a lot about being asked to join. Everyone in T.Au.M. is either pretty or smart or funny, and most of them are all three. You have to be asked to join by some girl coming up behind you and tapping you on the left shoulder and whispering to you, 'Piscem natare doces,' and the other day, this girl in the club came up and tapped me on the shoulder, and I turned around and looked at her and smiled, I was so happy. But she just wanted to borrow my *eraser. Now I don't care as much about joining T.Au.M. because I finally have a definite plan for St. Ursula's Girls Against the Atomic Bomb.*

I feel like I'll be creating something that wasn't there before. Someone once said it's never too late to become the person you were meant to be.

* *

Raine and Al went outside and sat on the bench in front of the school. It was a glorious day, with the leaves in the park across the street turning orange and gold. "I don't think St. Ursula's is such a bad place," she said.

"We try to be a galaxy of questioning minds, rather than a dogmatic academy focused on quantifiable achievements," he said. "Our girls come here to learn to think, not to memorize facts. We gather together to understand ambiguity, complexity, mystery, and paradox—not to deny they exist. Do you know who the patron saint of self-scrutiny is?"

"Galileo? Copernicus? Freud?"

"Socrates. His mother was a midwife. His father was a sculptor. He wore a shabby robe and went barefoot and loved to go to the marketplace and say, 'How many things there are here that I do not want!' Socrates felt that he was wiser than others only because he *knew* that he knew nothing. His method was for two people to try to agree about something minor and then slowly and gradually to creep together from truth to truth. In asking for definition, he could lead the other person into contradiction until the person's idea reshaped itself. So—if you're willing, Raine, we'll try to engage in a Socratic dialogue."

"My grandmother was in love with Freud," she said.

"Yes. You told me."

"It makes me mad that these new people moved into her apartment and took down the curtains and tore out the carpets."

"When did your grandmother meet Freud?" he said.

"In 1926. She was twenty-three and he was sixty-nine. She lived in Banska Stiavnica, north of Vienna, and she went to Freud's house after he had left for London and found a swastika flying over his door. But she said the Nazis couldn't get at him because he was the man who marched into a burning building as the rats were running out. He had a collection of wooden gods and marble horses on his desk and a couch made of horsehair. His beard smelled like hyacinths. She said he was one of the people who disturbed the sleep of the world. His eyes pierced through all sham and illusion."

"You have a lot of stories," he said. "And stories are a rich source of identity. Your parents came in to see me yesterday."

"They did?"

"Yes. I thought they were very nice."

"They are nice. They're very nice. Even though they're always trying to make me into a member of the pooch parade. Dr. Hadcock says their lives still revolve around a lot of Old World ideas. 'Children should not speak unless spoken to.' 'One word is enough to cause a lot of trouble.' 'Silence is golden.'"

Silence is golden? He wasn't sure he had ever met a student who talked as much as Raine.

* *

Raine was standing on her head in the window seat. Pavel was hanging by his legs from the branch of the dogwood tree outside her window. They were gazing into each other's eyes.

"What do you see?" she said.

"I see—I see...Wonder Woman fending off bullets with her bulletproof bracelets. What do you see?"

"The blue Danube," she said. "It's full of fish, and the fish are blossoming into flowers. Did you know fish lose their color when they die?"

"I really want to spend the day with you, Raine," he said.

"I know, but I'm having lunch with Daddy. He's trying to get to know me. And he isn't very fond of Slovakians. I explained to him that you and I are trying to strengthen new neurological pathways to the brain, but he wasn't very impressed."

"Guess what, Raine? I told my mom you're going away with me over Thanksgiving."

"Where are we going?"

"To Nebraska. To see a nuclear missile silo. You'll come with me, right?"

"I don't know, Pavel. I have a lot of studying to do. Lately, I've been feeling really grateful to my parents for having me. Maybe it's because my dad has been taking me out to lunch on Saturdays—to this vegetarian restaurant he hates—and it isn't exactly that he's growing on me. It's more like his *morals* are growing on me."

"If we grow up and do what our parents tell us to do, and they did what their parents told them to do, there won't be any human progress. Your morals should be growing on *him*."

"Can we get rightside up now?"

"No. Not until one of us has a revolutionary idea. Something that's never been thought before."

"What do you think of me, Pavel?"

"I like you, Raine. You're a nice person."

"Do you think love is a feeling you have about somebody? Or is it a bunch of sacrifices you make for them?"

"*Please*—no lugubrious Romeo and Juliet talks," he said. "Why are you always so serious?"

"I don't know."

Pavel dropped to the ground. "I'm a magical manifestation of infinity!" he called up to her.

She dropped out of her headstand and leaned out the window. She loved to think about Wonder Woman getting her lasso around an octopus and compelling it to tell the truth.

* *

The police station smelled of green peppers. Taped to the malt-colored walls were posters of the F.B.I. Most Wanted Criminals. The sergeant was glaring at Al. A half-eaten meatball submarine sat on the orange Formica desk. "What's wrong with this kid?" he said. "Is she buzzed or what?"

"She doesn't think anything's wrong with her," Al said. "She thinks something's wrong with the world."

"She listed you as next of kin."

"I am *not* next of kin. She has parents. When they're out of town, the housekeeper is in charge of her. You've dragged her in before—you should know that. I'm the school guidance counselor. My hours are seven-thirty to four."

The sergeant took a bite of his sandwich. "You haven't done much of a job guiding her, have you?"

"Believe me, I've tried."

"Don't cloud up and rain all over me, pal. We're interested in murderers and felons, not high school girls chaining themselves to flagpoles."

"Don't arrest them then."

"She broke the law. Get it? If I see her in here again, I'm gonna put your head in the toilet."

Al said nothing to Raine as he signed the papers and they walked together into the street. He flagged down a taxi, and once they were settled into the backseat, he said, "So what's so attractive about the 25th Precinct? Is it the O'Henry bars in the vending machines?"

"It's the purity of a moral act. I believe that getting arrested is very American. Debating, experimenting, disobeying, being restless and dissatisfied with things as they are."

Al tried to remain calm. "You don't have any plans," he said. "You don't have any friends. Where are you headed, Raine?"

"Into oblivion like the rest of us. Oblivion might arrive early, though. One day I might be in the cafeteria eating the tuna fish sandwich that got zapped with the radioactive waste some bozo dumped in the sea. And I won't even know it."

"On the one hand, you're fearless. You don't mind getting arrested. On the other hand, your fears dominate and paralyze you. Can't you see that? What began as a little pile of demerits is becoming a criminal record. You talk a lot about destructiveness, but when do you do anything constructive?"

"St. Veronica used to clean the floor with her tongue, so I guess I can sit here a little longer listening to you express your opinions about my life."

"Hearing the truth isn't what you're accustomed to, is it?" he said.

"Guess what, Mr. K? You're a cockroach. You're going

to survive a nuclear war."

* *

Finally, I'm a citizen—I've been arrested! Everyone is furious. Mother was in Prague, Daddy was in Washington, Mary was out, so Mr. K. had to come up to the 25th Precinct to fetch me, and he was NOT pleased. I gave him a long lecture about Thoreau going to jail, and Emerson coming and saying, "Henry, what are you doing in there?" and Thoreau saying, "Ralph, what are you doing out there?" I pointed out to him that Socrates was imprisoned, but he doesn't really care about Socrates' ideas—he just seems to be interested in my receiving a piece of parchment stating that I am an educated person. I don't really want to be a disappointment to anyone, but I'm proud of myself for listening to my inner voice and taking action. Of course, I demonstrate at the military academy every week, and I've never gotten arrested before—that's because the security guard Dave (who apparently finds me a refreshing presence in that environment of mold) was on vacation. He went kayaking in North Carolina with his brother-in-law, and his replacement was not awfully interested in the dangers of nuclear annihilation. I gave him one of my mini-lectures—and he responded by calling the police. What nerve! I informed him that I had been respectfully demonstrating at the military academy for many weeks and had earned my squatter's rights—however, he did not seem well-versed on

*the law. I've always wondered if I'd have the courage to do
something like this, but if I had known I was actually going
to be arrested, would I have gone home instead? Anyway,
the issue is this: the law and I have to take a look at each
other and figure out which one of us has to move. I
explained this in great detail to the police sergeant. He was
no comprende.*

*"At last, in a world torn by the hatreds and wars of men,
appears a woman to whom the problems and feats of men are
mere child's play. She is known only as Wonder Woman, but
who she is, or whence she came, nobody knows."*

* *

He wanted to be nice to Raine, but he could feel his
anger building. He tried to relax by looking at the portrait of
the calm-faced, rosy-cheeked St. Ursula on his office wall.
Raine was sitting across from him, peeling off her nail polish.

"Do you know you're the first student I've *ever* had to
retrieve from the police station?" he said. "If you want to
leave St. Ursula's, *leave*. Please. You're almost eighteen years
old. Find yourself a window and crawl through it, since we
all know you're not conventional enough to walk through a
door. Save us all the aggravation you're putting us through.
Help us conserve *some* of our energy for our other students."

"I apologize for being an individual and not a flock of
sheep," she said.

"Your grades have been decent—but frankly, Miss

Rassaby, I'm finding you increasingly uncooperative."

"Thank you. I consider that a compliment. Being agreeable in this society is a good way of getting nuked to the Pleiades."

"Would you mind imposing some boundaries on your concerns before they grow completely out of control?"

"Adults always act like they're Gepetto, and they're afraid someone else is going to breathe life into Pinocchio."

Water was gurgling in the gutters. A long silver cloud was hanging over the river. He tried to compose himself, then he turned to her and said, "Talk about a peaceful world, Raine—you are a *conflict*-generator!"

"You know what, Mr. K.? I'm glad you're not always nice to me. It would make for a very Anglo-Saxon relationship."

He sat down at his desk and counted out three breaths. "Let's try some relaxation techniques," he said. "Do you want to? Close your eyes. Take a deep breath."

She closed her eyes.

"What do you see?" he said.

"I see polar bears saying goodbye to us. I see snow leopards. I see grizzly bears. I see jaguars. I see giant ibises. I see whooping cranes. I see tiger cats. I see California pronghorn antelopes. They're waving."

He strolled over to the window. The weather was clearing. The sun was a blur of gold in the mist. "You're always talking about people considering the consequences of their actions, but when do you consider the consequences of *your* actions?" he said. "I'm getting tired of your obsession with bombs."

She stood up and said, "You don't seem to like it that I do what I think is right and not what you think is right, but if you don't want to listen to me talk about *bombs*, you better get some earplugs because nobody's ever told me what to talk about and nobody's ever going to. And I happen to like to talk about BOMBS, BOMBS, BOMBS because people like you are a little dead from the neck up and you have to say it a lot: BOMBS BOMBS BOMBS BOMBS BOMBS BOMBS!"

* *

Al decided to see, firsthand, what Raine was up to on Thursday afternoons, so he walked up to 110th Street and watched her lying across the doorway of the Mt. Abrams Military Academy in her skeleton costume. Hesitantly, he walked up the path toward her. A young man in a khaki uniform stepped over her and said, "That's just the way I like my women—lying down!" Then he walked away, laughing.

Al looked down at her. She seemed so small and vulnerable, lying there in her ridiculous costume. What kind of a path was she on? He had read that "Sabotage and Malicious Destruction of Property of the United States" were charges that could send her to prison for twenty years. He stepped closer to her and said, "What are you doing, Miss Rassaby?"

"Oh, hi, Mr. K. What are you doing here?" Her voice was muffled beneath her mask.

"We had an agreement. Remember?"

"You know where these guys are headed?" she said. "Into the Air Force. Air *Force*. Couldn't they have found a more attractive name?"

"Get *up*, Raine," he said. "Now."

"Okay." She stood up and slipped off her mask. Her hair was a mass of golden fuzz.

"What do you have against the military academy?" he said. "You must agree that some wars are justified."

"The problem is, it just seems so easy to have a war. Then that war creates more wars."

"You chose to come to St. Ursula's. Why can't a young man choose to come here?"

"Because they're choosing not to be an individual, which is too much of a luxury in a dangerous world like this one."

"Guess what, Raine. The next time I see you dressed as a skeleton, it better be Halloween. The future is on its way, and you don't have a practical thought in your head about it."

"Will there even be a future? The Cold War is over, but Russia and the U.S. still have all these nuclear weapons. I don't have a lot of admiration for pessimists, but still—I find it hard to be hopeful. But then I think that all Homo sapiens alive today come from a long series of ancestors, and every one of them was smart enough to survive."

"I'm trying to get through to you," he said. "But nothing I say seems to make much of an impression." Students were streaming past them. He tried to regain his composure. "Are you looking for another skirmish with the police?"

"If you'll excuse me, I believe my stamp collection is coming unglued," she said, turning her back to him. He plunged his hands into his pockets and began pacing around the statue of General Omar Bradley. She felt like running away, but she made herself stand there and watch the boys in uniform trail off down the street. She longed to shout at Al, "You wear pants of dogskin!" But instead she gave herself a lecture. Hadn't becoming a bat mitzvah meant anything? Hadn't she taken on new responsibilities at that ceremony? When was she going to shower the world with kindness? When was she going to start performing the 613 *mitzvahs?*

"The shaman's primary allegiance is to the supernatural dimension, not the society," she said when Al stopped pacing. "The bat mitzvah is a path to a summit."

They walked silently toward West 89th Street. "I guess I can understand why young people would be frightened of nuclear weapons," he said when they reached his street.

"How come you're not frightened, too?"

He wasn't sure why. "I suppose St. Ursula's could consider having air raid drills again," he said. "Then if a nuclear bomb is ever dropped, you'll be prepared. You'll know what to do."

"That's right," she said. "I'll vaporize."

* *

Two places were set in front of the kitchen window. Linen napkins were folded beneath each set of forks. The room smelled of tomato soup and horseradish. Al sat down and looked out the window at the trail of orange berries weaving along the Rassabys' fence. The sunflowers in the garden were drooping. He watched the goldfinches feasting on thistle seed as Raine lay in her hammock, singing.

Every Saturday, he ate the lunch Frieda cooked for them, then washed the dishes, scoured the oven and stove, locked the bathroom door and sank with book in hand into a tub of steaming water to emerge an hour later—Saturday after Saturday, year after year—with soft rumpled skin and a deep feeling of well-being.

But today, Frieda seemed distant and dreamy as she brought the steaming bowls of soup and potatoes to the table and sat down across from him.

"So how's it going at work?" he said.

"I have too much to do, as usual, but I love working with my old friends. They're such great human beings. I learn a lot from them."

"You and that social worker seem to have a nice relationship," he said.

"His name's Daniel. You always call him 'that social

worker.'"

"You and Daniel, then."

"We've been reading the Bible together for fifteen minutes before work."

Al wasn't sure how to respond. Could reading the Bible with Daniel possibly be as unwholesome as it sounded? "It's nice he invited you to go biking," he said.

"You don't mind, do you?"

"No," he said. "Did he stay late and help you put your patients to bed last night?"

"No, but he stays when he can. He doesn't have much of a life. He hates to go home. I guess it's lonely for him. He hasn't met his mate, but I always tell him, as soon as the right one comes along, he'll know it."

"Remember when we met?" Al said.

She smiled. "You walked up and handed me a plate of strawberries."

"No I didn't. I walked up and kissed you."

"No you didn't," she said. "I would have hated it if you had. I don't like men to take liberties they should have to earn."

"I handed you a plate of strawberries?" he said.

"You were offering me your heart. I knew it right away. It was very sweet."

"I knew it right away too," he said. "Isn't that strange? My first look at you. Of course, I looked at you for a while."

"An hour and a half," she said.

"There was something about you. It was your eyes, but it was more than that, too."

"It was love," she said.

"It still is, Frieda."

"Really? You seem so—"

"I know."

After lunch, he wanted to smooth his hands down over Frieda's sun-warmed hair. He longed to put his arm around her and lead her into their bedroom and share everything he was thinking with her and ask her a lot of questions and make love to her. Instead, he sat gazing out the window, listening to Mrs. Rassaby running through the scales on her violin. He watched a flock of grosbeaks fly into the garden and peck at the withered sunflowers. Robins mated for life. But he was sure they did not return to the nest every night with tales to tell their mate of a dazzling peacock.

* *

Raine and Pavel decided to have a Seder in her bedroom, even though it was not Passover. She bought six yellow tulips for the table, a reminder of the Dutch resistance and, Pavel said, of the best and worst in human beings. He brought some carrots and potatoes, a reminder of Slovakia, and a bottle of Manischewitz. Raine brought a bone from the butcher's, potato pancakes from the Broadway Delicatessen, matzos, a hard-boiled egg, parsley, salted water, *haroseth*, two brass candlesticks, a pot of tea, and honeycake to signify a sweet year. Pavel read the Passover story from the *Haggadah*. Raine asked the Four Questions.

The sun was setting, and she could hear a bird singing outside the window with a dull metallic *tick, tick, tick*. Her head was spinning from the sweet wine. They were sitting cross-legged on the floor, with the table—a cardboard box covered with yellow damask—and the vase of tulips between them.

"You can graft the branch of the peach tree onto the cherry tree, but it will still grow cherries," Pavel said.

Raine felt she should say something, so she said, "A Jew is full of hope. It's our nature."

"The Bal Shem Tov said, 'Forgetting is exile and remembering is redemption.'" Pavel smiled at her. She liked being alone with him.

"You have a beautiful face," she said. "When you smile at me—I can't describe how I feel."

"Tell me," he said.

"I don't know. I feel happy."

From his worn leather prayer book, they read the prayers together. Their secret world was Slovakia—the wild violets, the blackout drills, the rations, the castle ruins, the trains transporting Jews to the camps. They held hands and she told him the story of Ruth and Naomi. The candles burned down, sputtering and flickering in the breeze. Raine moved over beside him, put her arm around him, closed her eyes, and listened as Pavel read to her from the Book of Arguments. Fifty years separated them from the war. But during their Seder, she understood that they were not like other people, and she wondered if they would ever feel safe.

* *

October 25, 1998

I can't believe it—as of today—da-dum, da-dum, pum-pum-pum—I'm eighteen years old. Finally, I'm the brains in charge of my own life. I started out the day in the garden trying to play "Happy Birthday" on my bagpipes and imagining the neighbors flinging open their windows to wish me a happy adult life. Instead, from all directions, I was met with a cascade of grumpiness that I tried not to let contaminate the occasion. It's practically impossible to figure out how to live as an adult. What exactly do I believe, and how do I get my beliefs aligned with my actual life? Mother and Daddy gave me a check for $500, which was very nice of them. I tried to look happy when I opened it, but I felt really crestfallen because I was hoping they'd pick out something for me. Mary, who makes me feel like the peanut butter between two slices of bread, gave me a new pair of earmuffs.

* *

On the anniversary of Vikey's death, Raine's mother was

on a concert tour, her father was working, and Pavel did not respond to her invitation, so Raine held the *yahrzeit* service with Mary in the garden. On the evening before, she put photographs of Vikey around a white candle in her room, lit the candle, and prayed that it would burn all night.

She loved the sensible Jewish tradition of getting angry about death and knew that if she wanted, she could stomp on Vikey's grave, or rip up some of her clothes. But during the year since her death, she had found it too sad even to open her box of Vikey's clothes.

Each day, she had said *Kaddish* for Vikey—the mourner's prayer that never mentioned death but only talked about the glory of God's creation. And she had tried to focus on their good times together—all the bus rides to the Cloisters or down to the Staten Island ferry, all the meals at the Italian Kitchen on 42nd Street and the times they had ridden the carousel and ice-skated and fed sugar lumps to the horses outside Central Park. They had gone to Aqueduct Racetrack, the Brooklyn Trolley Museum, Radio City Music Hall, the Ellis Island Wall of Honor, the Center for Jewish History, El Museo del Barrio, Astroland Amusement Park, and the Empire State Building. Raine had loved spending time with Vikey, but she doubted that she had ever truly expressed her appreciation.

So at the *yahrzeit* service in the garden, in the freezing cold, while she and Mary sat on two chairs facing the brick wall covered with dead vines, with the *yahrzeit* candle lit between them, she said, "Thank you for taking me everywhere, Vikey. Thank you for listening to me. Thank you for listening to your courageous voice instead of your fearful one. Thank you for being an example to me. Thank you for being a heroine. I'm sorry I didn't call you. I'm sorry I didn't say goodbye to you. *Zichronah livrachah*."

II

"I do appreciate you taking me out to lunch every Saturday, Daddy. It's really sweet. It makes me want to cry."

"My pleasure, Raine," he said.

"I hope you're not embarrassed to be seen with me," she said.

She was wearing a wrinkled black dress, an olive green wool hat, one white sock and one red sock, and a pair of unlaced combat boots.

"Maybe you can get Mary to iron some of your clothes," he said.

"I would, Daddy, but I met this Hindu in the street who said that ironing causes a cruel death to the tiny mites living in the fabric."

He reached across the table and took her hand. "I'm sitting here thinking that I'm a fifty-four-year-old man with a grown daughter and a big stack of eighty-hour weeks piled up behind him."

"You shouldn't have any regrets, Daddy. I think you've been a fine father. You really tried to believe in me. Remember how you used to send me to space camp?"

"You hated it," he said.

"I loved meeting the astronauts, and I liked your deluding yourself into thinking I might be smart enough and brave enough to become an astronaut."

"We should have spent the summers with you when you were little—not gone off on vacations and sent you away to camp."

"Remember cooking camp? I learned to make fish stock and chocolate dacquoise."

"We felt Mary needed some time off in the summer."

"Remember Camp Tonawanga? There was an epidemic of encephalitis."

"I remember them all," he said.

She loved the way the sunlight was shining through the glass of carrot juice on the table and glinting on her father's gold cuff link. "There's this part of me that's very weak and doesn't know much and is scared of everything," she said. "But under it is something else, this strong person who believes in the power of love and thinks human beings can squirm out of their predicaments. One layer is full of fear and one layer is full of belief. Do you ever feel like that?"

"Of course. It's the human condition."

"It is?"

"I like the way you labor over everything, Raine. It's a wonderful trait. I was thinking this morning how Mary used to dye the bread pink and blue on your birthdays to make sandwiches for your parties. I always hated coming downstairs in the morning and seeing those little pastel sandwiches with the crusts cut off because that meant you were another year older. You can't imagine how fast the years go." He refilled her teacup and said, "May I say something honestly?"

"You might as well."

"Raisa and I feel you spend too much time looking for things to be unhappy about."

"It's more like they look for me."

"A certain amount of good and a certain amount of evil will always be present in the world. So it's a matter of what you choose to look at. My parents left Slovakia before I was born. It was a dangerous place to live, even for Christians. And your mother lived there, under the Nazis, for the first six years of her life. I often wonder what that was like for her. When I first met her, I could see that there was a great deal of feeling in her—all that emotion she invested in her music. I used to sit in the back row at her rehearsals. I stayed for hours, listening. I was mesmerized by her violin. Perhaps she was telling her audience what it was like to be a child living in a land where people were being exterminated. She was the one who used to take food out to the Jews Vikey had hidden. I wonder what that was like."

"She won't talk about it," Raine said. "Maybe I'm picking up all the horrible stuff she's repressing. Did you ever think of that?"

"You're trying to understand something that's impossible to understand. We're all like that, to some extent. We don't understand what happened. We *can't* understand."

"So you fell in love with Mother's music?"

"Yes," he said. "Even before I met her."

"That's exactly what happened to me—I heard Pavel playing the *gajdy* at that first picnic, and I felt like a rat running after the Pied Piper. Daddy, I think I've finally learned the difference between infatuation and love. With infatuation, you go around really excited but really insecure all the time, and with love, you walk around thinking that the universe is beautiful, people are good, civilization is improving, and love can move mountains."

"I hope you always believe that," he said.

"Daddy, you know how people have things like coming-out parties? Or bat mitzvahs—like the one Vikey planned for me that you chose not to attend?"

"Yes," he said.

"I don't think I should just go from being a kid to an adult without having some kind of serious celebration. Remember when I got my period, and you bought me a dozen roses?"

"Yes I do," he said, smiling.

"That's kind of what I'm talking about."

"A celebration, you mean?"

"A trip," she said.

"A trip?"

"To Nebraska."

"To Nebraska?" he said.

"A trip to Nebraska with Pavel."

"This is your second run at senior year, Raine. Time to stop fooling around."

"*Please,* Daddy. It would be a very serious trip. We wouldn't be going to have fun. You go on a trip like that to face yourself and find out what you're made of. It's a long trip, and you don't sleep. It's kind of like going to a Native American sweat lodge."

"Raine, you're being very cryptic. Can you just say what you want?"

"We get a week off from school at Thanksgiving, and I want to go to Nebraska with Pavel to see a nuclear missile silo."

"You can't see nuclear missile silos. They're underground. And I don't understand the coming-of-age part."

"Because I want to go away with Pavel, and I'm nervous about asking you. You and I have kind of an infantile relationship, only because up 'til now I've been a child and you've been a parent."

"And a trip to Nebraska's going to change that?" he said.

"It will be kind of a cleaver. After I come back, you and I will be more like two adults."

"Raine, if you want to be an adult, you don't need a trip. You need a diploma. And a job. I admire all your enthusiasms, dear. I really do. But I have a feeling Pavel is not what you need right now. Every good relationship needs a sail and a keel, and you and Pavel are two sails. You need to spend Thanksgiving break studying."

"Are you just not mentioning the unmentionable?" she said.

"What would that be?"

"*Sex.*"

"Going away for a week with a young man? I imagine it would be an issue."

"Because Pavel is sort of bashful and retarded in that department, if that's what you're worried about. You'll be happy to know."

"That's probably good news, in this day and age."

"We're also quite nervous about the specter of H.I.V."

"As well you should be," he said.

"So can I go?"

"*May* I go?" he said.

"Yeah."

"No, you may not."

* *

"Our first meeting of St. Ursula's Girls Against the Atomic Bomb is in the park on Saturday," Raine said to Al.

"There isn't a lamppost in the neighborhood that isn't plastered with the news. I take it you're working on this club instead of studying."

"It isn't exactly a club. It's more of a revolution, hopefully. There are eight million residents in New York, so I figure if one half of one percent come to our meeting, that's forty thousand people."

"Don't get your hopes up, Raine. People may not feel like thinking about our nuclear stockpile on Saturday. They're predicting good weather. My wife is going biking."

"Frieda's a biker?"

"This guy at work talked her into trying it," he said. He hated talking about Frieda and Daniel. "If a handful of people come to your meeting, it will be a start."

"You'll be there, right?"

"Sorry. No. I have plans."

"Doing what?"

"I have some things to attend to."

"If I were you, I'd go biking with Frieda and her paramour."

"He is *not* her paramour. He's a social worker at the nursing home. He's new in town and doesn't know many people. My compassionate wife has befriended him."

"How old is he?" she said.

"I think he's in his late twenties. He just got out of grad school. Frieda says he's nice."

"Nice guys do not finish last, Al. That's a myth."

"Is that nun coming to your meeting?"

"She says if you feed people, they'll come. She's bringing jelly doughnuts and coffee. Do you like jelly doughnuts?"

"No. I don't."

"Is anything more important than getting rid of nuclear weapons? Can I just ask you that?"

"I have a farm to take care of," he said. "I'm going up there on Saturday."

"You told me about it once. Did your grandmother bequeath it to you?"

"I guess so. She died very suddenly."

"Oh my God, we have karma! My grandmother died suddenly, too. Last year."

"I know she did. I'm sorry."

"My mother was a baby when Hitler marched into Slovakia and said, '*Mine!*' My grandmother really related to Jews, and she loved the religion, so she converted to Judaism when she came over here in 1946. I converted when I was thirteen. She was very, very attached to me, and I was very, very attached to her, but when Pavel came along, I started to ignore her. I didn't call her for three weeks. Then you know what happened? She died."

"I'm sorry, Raine."

"It was horrible. I'll never get over it. It was Halloween, and I always took her trick-or-treating. We wore the same costumes every year. She was dressed up as a princess, and I was a telephone, and we went around, just in her building since New Yorkers are not renowned for opening their door when someone knocks. She loved it when we went back and emptied our candy on the floor of her apartment and traded stuff. I let her have anything she wanted—even the Nestle's Crunches. But last year, I didn't call her because Pavel said we could go out on Halloween, but he never even called. I just sat by the phone. And the next day, she was dead."

"That's very sad," Al said, and after Raine left, he thought of his grandmother lying on the floor of the farmhouse kitchen, how he had discovered her and then run out into the woods. He had always dreamed—or more than dreamed, *known*—that one day, they would sit together and say exactly how they felt about each other. He could still picture them talking and laughing as they sat together in the creaking glider on the porch.

* *

At the first meeting of St. Ursula's Girls Against the Atomic Bomb, only she and Sister Claudette appeared, so Raine decided to hold the second meeting at school in the media room. That afternoon, she paced up and down in the hall, waiting for someone to appear. She had written a speech, which she planned to deliver in a lofty and ardent voice, keeping everyone spellbound. But she wasn't sure she could do it. She closed her eyes and hoped she wouldn't be the only one at the meeting, and when she opened them, she saw a girl with red hair and freckles hurrying toward her down the hall. "Is this where the meeting is?" the girl said. She had eyes like green quartz.

"Yes," Raine said.

"Great. I like the name of the group. It's musical."

"You mean you want to join?" Raine said.

"Sure."

"Do you know anyone else who does?"

"My friends are coming," the girl said.

"They are? Really?"

The girl put out her hand and said, "I'm Janey. You're new here, right?"

"Right. I'm Raine."

"You just moved to New York?"

"No, I was born here. But I flunked out of Horace Mann last year, so I'm giving this place a try."

"Good for you," Janey said. "Welcome to St. Ursula's. Was the group your idea?"

"Yes. I want people to feel like I do, but I don't know what to say to get them to."

"About nuclear weapons, you mean?"

"Yeah. I think about them all the time."

"Really?" Janey said. "Say that, then. Just tell people how you feel." Janey squeezed her arm and walked into the room.

Her whole life had prepared her for this moment. Instead of just being afraid of nuclear weapons, it was time to start protesting them. This day reminded her of her bat mitzvah ceremony, when she went up to the *bimah*, and her voice shook as she started to sing, and then gradually, her chanting got stronger and louder and more beautiful, and for the first time in her life, she felt close to God.

* *

We had our second meeting of St. Ursula's Girls Against the Atomic Bomb, and I was disappointed to discover that I am not an orator. My speeches are not impassioned like Helen Caldicott's or Hitler's even though I feel the passion. I just can't express it. It's all this stuff that's clogged inside me like sap, and it refuses to burst forth. I cannot think in public. I'm not sure what the problem is. Still, the group is becoming quite successful. We have eighteen members.

This morning, I got up and I didn't feel like getting dressed, and I wondered what it would be like to go to school in my pajamas. I never minded walking through the streets in my skeleton costume because I was wearing a mask, so I could see people without them seeing me. I was hiding underneath the mask, like a mushroom growing in the dark. But wearing my pajamas in the street, dressed as me, seemed different. I want to be like everyone else, in a way. And this is a very mammally way to be—a way to survive. But if we keep banding together, it might be very bad, very very very bad, for Homo sapiens. I dream of living in a nuclear missile silo turned into an elongated house, but dreams are like balloons—they pop.

The members of St. Ursula's Girls Against the Atomic Bomb are talking about a dumb lecture series, when I wanted us to be more like Simone Weil parachuting into France to join the Resistance. But I made a stupid speech, and now Janey is becoming our leader. I guess it's true that some wells you fall down you never come up from.

Janey's mother's name is Kerunda. She actually approves of Janey rebelling against nuclear weapons. Is it possible that Kerunda and Raisa are members of the same generation? Oh my God, I'd be an entirely different person with a mother like that! Janey is such a great human being. I think she likes me, too. She's going to graduate, and she already got accepted at Princeton. The irony is that Kerunda wants Janey to go to astrology school. It is impossible to please parents—don't even try. I am the biggest parent-pleaser of all time. Making Dr. and Mrs. Rassaby happy takes up at least ninety percent of the beanbag room in my head where I fabricate my thoughts.

Why do nuns choose to become nuns and prostitutes choose to become prostitutes? Or don't either of them actively choose? One day when we were sitting on a bench on Broadway, my friend Wanda invited me to join her escort service, and that whole idea is startling but interesting—the amount of freedom I actually have and the amount I use. It's fascinating even to contemplate the exact expletives

*Mother and Daddy would use if I chose to let a man pay
five hundred dollars for the joy of spending an evening with
me. We're free, but we behave in certain ways because com-
pliance is the foundation of civilization. But isn't morality
that fine line between obedience and selfishness, a line I
think very few people try to find for themselves? They look
to books or other people to tell them where it is, but (in my
opinion) you have to flunk around in that gunk before you
know for sure whether you're doing right or wrong. Mr. K.,
the Mother Superior, and Mother and Daddy have an
agenda for me, but Pavel and Mary and Vikey want me to
blossom into this great flamboyant creature, Raine Marie
Rassaby, Crab Apple Queen of the Upper West Side. They
want for me the same thing the mice wanted for Cinderella.*

* *

"You can't go out like that," Karel said, holding open
the kitchen door and looking at Raine, who was about to
open the garden gate.

"What's the problem, Daddy?"

"You forgot to get dressed."

"I must wear my pajamas to school today for reasons it
would be too complicated to explain," Raine said.

He looked at his watch. "Okay," he said. "I see I'm
never going to change you. Wear a coat, at least."

"I think it would be cowardly to hide my pajamas
under a coat."

She followed him from the garden into the house, watched him put on his overcoat and scarf, walked him to the front door, kissed him goodbye, and closed the door behind him. Then she sat down on the couch and realized it was easier for her to break the law than to look like a fool. She slid her feet onto the coffee table and closed her eyes. She was just like other people—concerned about her image. She complained about uniforms, but at the same time, she was afraid to appear in public as she really was. She didn't want anyone to see the real girl under the false girl.

She walked into the kitchen where Mary was eating her breakfast and said, "Mary, did you really go into a cave to look for a bear?"

"Grandfather said there is always a bear hunt, even if there is no bear," Mary said.

Raine sat down across from her and said, "So what did you have to do to get ready for a bear hunt?"

"Work up my courage by talking to the ancestors."

Raine poked her head out the front door, looked both ways, and stepped outside. Her flannel pajamas were quite colorful—blue and orange stripes—and she felt good that they were clearly pajamas and that she had not weaseled out of the challenge by putting on a coat.

No one on West 88th Street paid any attention to her, and the nine blocks down Riverside Drive proved to be uneventful, too. People did not seem to notice that she was wearing her pajamas, maybe because New Yorkers had seen everything. Once she had seen a man walking down Broadway flossing his teeth.

She forced herself to look directly into several faces, but it was hard—like looking into the eyes of the dentist as he was working on her teeth. She had a feeling that when she went into St. Ursula's and walked down the hall, the Mother Superior would not be as blasé. Raine would have to explain to her that the time had come for mammals to branch off into individuality, and she was planning to lead the herd. Wolves lived in packs and banded together and were suspicious of otherness and variety, but dogs, who had evolved from wolves, had learned to be friendly. Had they learned this because someone had brought them inside, where they had to act friendly in order to be fed? Or had they been painstakingly trained out of their suspicious and aggressive traits? How exactly had it happened? How did change occur? Could people bring it about, or was progress inevitable, in spite of humanity? Did human beings, like animals, merely have to wait for it?

When she reached the school, she stopped, turned around, and walked home to change into her uniform.

* *

Raine and Pavel were sitting at the kitchen table, eating popcorn and ice cream. "I'm finally beginning to realize that I'm quite the conformist," Raine said. "And on top of that, I'm crazy. There's no health for someone with scrupulosity."

"Swear you won't say anything about being crazy when you come over for dinner."

"When am I coming over for dinner?"

"I don't know," he said. "Soon."

"Dr. Hadcock said scrupulosity isn't something to be ashamed of."

"She doesn't know my mother."

"She doesn't like me, right?"

"I told her you were hypersensitive and she had to watch what she said to you."

"I don't know if I like keeping my craziness a secret, Pavel."

"Why not?"

"Because then I have to go over to your house and act like someone I'm not. And that doesn't seem like a good idea because then I'll always have to worry that someday she'll figure out who I really am. Why should I try to hide part of my real self?"

"You shouldn't," he said. "But my dad's been dead fifteen years, and my mom doesn't have a life outside of me. She works, but after work, she always stops at the grocery store and comes straight home and starts cooking. She gets depressed if I don't show up for dinner. She doesn't even know I hang out down here. It's good to be honest, but you can't be completely honest with mothers. They're too possessive."

"My mother isn't possessive. I wish she was." She was carving Pavel's initials into the salt at the bottom of the popcorn bowl. The leaves were falling out of the dogwood tree and blowing against the French doors. "Can't I just come over and be myself and not worry about what I say?"

"No," he said.

"Why not?"

"You'll see when you get there."

"Vikey always said one lie leads to another, and one cruelty leads to another." He didn't seem to be paying attention. She threw a piece of popcorn at him and said, "Guess what? I asked Daddy if I can go to Nebraska, and I know he'll tell Mother. It's like announcing we're planning to have sex."

He leaned across the table and kissed her. "We're planning to have sex?" he asked.

"That's what it sounds like."

"Since when do you care what things sound like?" he said.

"Talking to my parents about sexuality is embarrassing, which is kind of dumb, I guess. But there are a lot of things we don't talk about—we're kind of WASPy for Jews—and that's the biggest one of all. When they say *Pavel*, it's like they're saying *Penis*."

"Parents are strange. They're in love with us, but we're not in love with them."

Raine thought of Karel and Raisa. Had they ever, even for a short time, been in love with her? "I'd be glad to come over for dinner, Pavel," she said. "But I definitely will *not* pretend to be normal."

* *

Raisa was lying on her bed with cucumber slices covering her eyelids as Raine paced around her bed.

"I *am* trying, Mother," she said.

"It's the people you're associating with."

"Like who?"

"Like Mary."

"What's wrong with Mary?"

"Nothing. She's wonderful. But I'm afraid she's become a role model for you, and she's a woman without ambitions."

"Mary is a hunter, Mother. She crawled into caves to kill polar bears and dragged them home for dinner. She has more courage than a whole subway car full of New Yorkers. Her greatest ambition is to *live*."

"I'm tired of hearing her singing like a broken-hearted fox," Raisa said. "And then there's Pavel. Doesn't he have any aspirations?"

"Pavel spends his time having very interesting conversations with plants."

"Who's that blonde I saw you sitting with up on Broadway?"

"Wanda?" Raine said. "She's a prostitute. A very intelligent one."

"Do you have any normal friends? With normal ambitions?"

"Wanda's working her way up to become a hostess on a cruise ship, and Pavel wants to create a better world."

Her mother removed the cucumber slices, sat up, and glared at Raine. "I can't imagine where you're going to end up," she said.

"You use your talent to create beautiful music, and I want to use my talent to create something, too—but I have a feeling my only talent is persistence."

"Persistence is not a talent."

"I loved it in World War II when Winston Churchill said, 'We shall defend our island, whatever the cost may be, we shall fight on the beaches, we shall fight on the land, we shall fight in the fields and in the streets, we shall fight in the hills; we shall never surrender!'"

"What are your *plans*, Raine?"

"Pavel and I are hoping to be the forgers of a new conscience for our species."

"Pavel, Pavel, Pavel!"

"What were you doing when you were my age?" Raine said.

"Working eight hours a day as a secretary and practicing the violin four hours a day so I could get into music school."

"And you did get in—with a scholarship, right? That must be where I got my persistence."

"Even if you graduate from St. Ursula's, do you think any college will admit you?"

"Probably not, since I have no intention of going to college. I've decided to become an anti-nuclear activist, Mother."

"I'm sure that pays very well," Raisa said.

"It does. You get to sleep well at night and take pride in the fact that you're being a voice for the voiceless, speaking up for the giraffes and the salamanders, to say nothing of the two hundred and fifty generations of human beings who are going to have to keep watch over our nuclear waste. I'm hoping to find a patron—someone rich who hates nukes but is too much of a couch potato to do anything about them."

Raisa was crying. Raine sat down on the side of the bed and put her arm around her. "I'm sorry I'm such a disappointment, Mother, but I'm trying to do better. Mr. Klepatar mentioned that maybe we could have these Socratic dialogues. It will help me to be a better thinker."

"For all your talk of turning over a new leaf, every time I come home, expecting to see you studying, I find you in the garden with that Slovakian!"

"Mother, please don't get so upset. I'm sure I'll do spectacular things at St. Ursula's. Don't just assume I'll continue on my path of dismal failure. I have a great deal of hope for myself."

* *

Al tried to imagine how he'd feel when Daniel Wadhams rang the buzzer. He had devised several speeches, but the words receded when he was confronted with the sight of Frieda clad in Spandex shorts and a too-tight nylon top imprinted with jagged fluorescent colors and Daniel, sleek as a snake in black biking shorts. Al eyed the matching bikes beneath the window, remembering Roy Rogers and Dale Evans parking their horses side-by-side before galloping off into the sunset.

"So how've you been, Al?" Daniel asked, shaking his hand and smiling at him with tallowy white teeth.

"Fine," Al said.

"Al's swamped at work," Frieda said. "I'm sure he could use a day to collapse."

"Maybe I'll go for a run in the park," Al said.

"*You?*" Frieda said.

"Who knows—it might be fun," he said.

"Why don't you come biking with us?" Daniel asked.

Al conjured up a gloomy tableau of himself pedaling behind Daniel and Frieda in their biking shorts and helmets, huffing and puffing to keep up with them like the little kid that the big kids are trying to shake.

"He loves to make resolutions about getting in shape," Frieda said, and Daniel laughed anemically, with a strange tweeting sound.

The three of them sat down at the kitchen table, but Al found it hard to listen to Daniel attempting to sound humble as he discussed his generosities as a social worker. He struck Al as amazingly sensitive, horribly talkative, and overly fond of his clients and himself. "Maybe we should get going?" he finally said. His buzz cut made his eyes stand out. He needed a shave, and the haze of fuzz made him look childishly manly. Al imagined him pedaling behind Frieda, gazing contentedly at her plump backside.

"'Bye, Al," Frieda said, clamping her helmet on.

"So long," Al said, closing the door behind them and heading for the window to watch them unlock the bikes on the sidewalk and push them determinedly into the morning fog. He could feel Frieda and Daniel slowly taking over his life, the way termites do, eating their way up through the joists, rafters, and floorboards until the house falls down.

A few leaves were left on the trees in the park; frost was glittering in the grass. Al imagined a male turtle swimming backwards beside a female, stroking and lightly tapping her face with his long fingernails. He could feel the autumn frenzy before winter set in, each species matching the best males with the worthiest females. Irresistible reactions were being triggered by internal clocks. The attraction of one for another was palpable in the air around him; how could it possibly be thwarted?

It was alarming to observe his fifteenth wedding anniversary approaching as his life seemed to be dividing itself into fourteen-year segments. Fourteen years with his mother in the boarding house; fourteen years with his grandmother on the farm; fourteen years with Frieda on West 89th Street.

A banner hanging above the pathway said: *Central Park: Thirty-Six Bridges to Kiss Under.* Sitting on a bench, he felt the cold metal slats under his thighs as bikers whizzed past him, the silver spokes of their wheels gleaming in the sun. The harvest was past, the time of abundance and gratitude, and now November, with its emptiness, its dankness, its bog of sorrows, was overpowering the golden beauty and promise of fall. Chipmunks and squirrels were grabbing acorns and nuts and running with them in every direction. Toads were trilling, snails were shooting love darts. But was it really love? Wasn't it something seamier and more elemental—like urgent necessity or wanton desperation?

Crackling, rust-colored leaves were falling from trees; tufts of wool clung to cinnamon ferns; the red-winged blackbirds were gone; a catbird was singing the cardinal's song.

Couples ran past him, bobbing up and down, sweating, heading home to bed. Even in the daylight, he could make out the flashing abdominal lamps of zigzagging creatures. Monarch butterflies lilted through the air, tiny black scent patches swelling on their wings. He thought of ritualized courtships, low croonings, male rats singing haunting post-ejaculation songs. If his wife rode by with that social worker, he would just have to stand up and start screaming.

Al's grandmother taught him that a circle of bark sliced from the trunk of a barren apple tree would stun the tree back into production, so he decided to go home and make a list of the things that would startle his marriage back to life. But walking past the lovers in Sheep Meadow sitting together on the orange grass, all he could picture was Daniel arriving on his bike, roping Frieda's suitcase on the rack, and decamping with her to his apartment in Spanish Harlem. Al would be incapable of living alone in their apartment. He'd go to the pound and adopt a cat. He'd return to his daily infusions of Scotch, get fired from his job, lose his home and his farm, and he and the cat would end up living in the sewer pipes under Broadway, being handed a sandwich and a can of cat food by none other than Daniel Wadhams.

As Frieda slipped away from him, she became more and more beautiful, wonderful, kind, and extraordinary— the consummate companion, the perfect wife.

* *

Al was shaving in the bathroom when Frieda came in and called out, "Al? Where are you?" He chose not to answer. He was busy thinking about protozoa reproducing by dividing themselves in two but then paying an exorbitant price for their sexual tranquility. The bathroom door opened, and Frieda popped her head in.

"Did you have fun?" he said.

"Daniel talked me into training for the triathlon."

"Terrific," he said. He wanted her to close the door. He wanted to stay in the bathroom. He thought of a garden with an impossibly narrow gate, a place to escape from grave thoughts, hedges of nuts and plums and quinces, puffs of acacia, green woodpeckers and blue warblers, a grove of trees where wild creatures could come to hide. The scent of Frieda was embedded in the moist, misty air of the bathroom. It was a coconut oil-tropical island smell, not the flowery fragrances she often doused herself in, presumably for Daniel. He opened the cupboard in search of perfume bottles. There weren't any. Maybe the smell was coming out of her pores?

Although Frieda was talkative, she revealed very little. The silence between them was becoming more noticeable. Just a word would allow them to break free of it—but it needed to be a word of truth. And which of them had the courage to utter that?

"Daniel has a hot date tonight," Frieda said at the dinner table. They were eating in the kitchen. If they had a dining room, if they actually *dined*, drinking wine by candlelight and talking to each other about their feelings, would their marriage be warmer? Would it be more fun? "I had to give him some pointers," she added.

"What kind of pointers?"

"Oh, you know. Ask questions. Don't make statements. Don't spend the evening talking about yourself. Tell her she looks nice."

His reflection was shining up at him out of the oak table. "What if she doesn't look nice?" he said.

"She will."

"What else?"

"Figure out if there's something he might be able to do for her. It feels great when you guys do something for us that isn't expected and isn't an obligation."

"Right," he said.

"Be attuned to her. Notice things. Be sensitive. Try to center in on who she really is, what's interesting and unique about her. And forget the bed stuff. It ruins relationships."

"You talk to Daniel about sex?"

"We talk about dating."

"I'm planning to cook dinner for us tomorrow night," he said.

"Really?"

"You'll have a hot bath, I'll give you a massage, then we'll have a glass of champagne and eat everything you love."

"I should go biking more often," she said.

"I want to take you to Bermuda next summer. To celebrate our fifteenth anniversary."

"I can't believe it will be fifteen years."

"It's a long time," he said. "We used to—" Odd the way he couldn't talk to her—but she could talk to Daniel—about sex. Still, she got the point.

"You're always so nervous," she said.

"But not because of you. It's, it's...."

He thought of a sea star resting on the tip of her arms, shielding her clump of eggs. He thought of a female water bug cementing a raft of eggs onto the male's back, and the male sinking, immobilized and suffocating, to the bottom of the pond. "Some people hate spiders," he said. "Some people hate snakes. Some people hate elevators. I hate babies. I always have."

"What's to hate about a baby!"

"Try to think of the most fabulous meal you can imagine," he said.

"Really?"

"Yes. I'm not kidding. Just describe it to me. I'll go shopping in the morning while you're at Mass."

"Let's see. Escargot in butter sauce. Mushroom soup

made with organic cream and gill-less chanterelles. You have to get them at Zabar's. Chicken marsala with broccoli rabe, sweet potatoes topped with marshmallows, a salad with cilantro and slivered almonds—you have to boil them, then rub the skins off. And brussels sprouts with lemon sauce. Hazelnut coffee, truffles, and a chocolate croquembouche."

"Maybe we could order takeout?" he said, and they laughed.

* *

Raine was in Al's office, watching him talking on the phone. She was thinking about the way Mary seemed to be floating away. She thought of a balloon being held in the gooey hand of a two-year-old, who suddenly lets it go. She could picture the balloon drifting up into the trees, then into the clouds. When Al put the phone down, she said, "Mary used to part my hair in the middle and paint a yellow streak down my scalp with some cattail pollen to keep me from getting struck by lightning, which made me feel safe, but after I turned thirteen, she didn't do that any more. For a while I was in love with Michael Ignaszewski and Patty White. Neither of them even knew I existed, but we all went to religious school together at St. Christopher's. I hated studying the New Testament. I liked Jesus' words, but I hated turning my back on the Torah, pretending I wasn't a Jew. And the nuns were always filling me up with what they wanted me to know, which felt like a form of advertising. Eventually, I got kind of fixated on Patty, and I loved Michael's white shirts and his turquoise eyes, but then something sad happened. One day I was sitting on a bench on Broadway feeding chocolate-covered raisins to the pigeons, and I saw Michael and Patty walking together up Broadway. I stood up and stared at them. They weren't holding hands, but every once in a while, they'd bump shoulders. They didn't see me or anyone else—they only saw each other—and it was their obliviousness that was so painful to watch because I wanted so much to have that kind of obliviousness with somebody. I walked home like I was sleep-walking and went up the stairs to my bedroom and climbed into bed and felt how completely separate I was from everyone and everything."

"So were you in love with this girl?"

"I guess I was doing what all girls do—shopping for a woman to become."

"Does Dr. Hadcock ever mention your obsession with evil?" he said.

"I think it's good to be obsessed. An obsession is a warm place you can crawl into."

They sat listening to the foghorns on the river.

"Do you think it would be a better world if nobody ever broke any laws?" she asked.

"There wouldn't be any crime."

"There wouldn't be any protests either. No matter what kind of law was passed, you'd have to obey it. What if there weren't any dreams. Oh my God—chop off my head right now!"

"It starts with a *g*, Raine, and it ends with an *n*, and everybody there is wearing a cap and gown. I know it's hard for you to stay focused, but I honestly think you can do it."

"I might just go my own way instead—writing my own music about things that are bothering me."

"You mean like nuclear weapons?" he said.

"I mean like the air I breathe, and the PCBs in my ovaries. Last night I read this great story of a woman in Holland during the Holocaust who decided to have a baby just because she was a Jew, and the Jews were being killed, so she got pregnant, and she found a Christian family to take the baby and pretend it was theirs. Isn't that beautiful?"

"There are a lot of fifteen-year-olds out there pushing baby carriages. It isn't a beautiful sight."

"Yeah," she said. "Making babies is what's cool now for kids my age, but we need to make something else. Like a better world." She got up and paced around for a while, then she said, "Mary used to gaze in the river in complete silence, for the longest time, waiting to hear from her ancestors. When I was little, we walked down to the river and stared into the water every day at noon. I'll never forget that time. Once, I wanted to break my mother's violin in two, but now I'm glad she has something in her life she's excited about. Do you have anything you're passionate about?"

"Passion is an excess—an imbalance," he said dreamily.

"What would you do if the Hlinka Guard knocked on your door someday?"

"Who?"

"The Nazis in Slovakia."

"What would I do?"

"Yeah."

"It would depend on what they wanted," he said.

"They'd want you to inform on the Jews—and they might kill you if you didn't."

"I'd want to do the heroic thing, and I don't know if I could live with myself afterward if I didn't. But I doubt if I'd have the courage. What would you do?"

"I guess that's the question, isn't it?"

Someone dropped a tray in the cafeteria down the hall. Then the bell rang and she jumped up, grabbed her backpack, and said, "*Hasta la vista,* Mr. K!"

He went home and looked for Frieda, but of course she was still at work. He wondered where betrayed lovers could go—even the ones who were imagining their betrayals, or facilitating them. He went into his den and made a list:

My virtues: loyalty
                   love of women
                   straight arrow

Daniel's virtues:	athletic
	manly
	compassionate
	young
My faults:	wary of men
	unappreciative
	becoming like Hamlet
	heading for a fall
Daniel's faults:	bold
	full of himself
	overly enthusiastic
	sugar-coated
	empathy to the brink of falseness

* *

Mr. Jezuliana was in the garden raking leaves and cutting back shrubs. He couldn't seem to stop singing. The snipping sound of his clippers followed the cadence of his song.

Mary set down a plate of cookies on the kitchen table, and Raine said, "If Mr. Jezuliana asked you to marry him and go off somewhere, what would you say?"

"I'd say Raine won't let me," Mary said.

"After Pavel leaves, I think about him all the time, and I feel sort of insecure. Is that how you feel about Mr. Jezuliana?"

"People from Greenland think it's funny to talk about love," Mary said.

"So you *do* love him! But he's so quiet. Do you know he never says hello to me?"

"When he comes over, we like to listen to the birds sing."

"And I'm sure you like to do more than that but you're not telling me because Greenlanders don't talk. It makes me very uncomfortable the way you always listen to your ancestors, Mary, especially when they're bugging you to go back to Greenland. Do you want to live your life according to what dead people think?"

"Raine, you are an American and you believe in the world of the living and the world of the dead. But in Greenland, we believe there is only one world."

Raine extracted the chocolate chips from her cookie, ate them, and wondered how Mary could possibly believe in one world when it seemed to her that there were so many worlds. "I love standing next to Pavel," she said. "I don't exactly hear bells, but everything inside me is going *clang*."

"At least you share an interest in atomic bombs," Mary said.

"I know what the poets mean when they say you get picked up and you fly on gossamer wings."

"What goes up always comes down," Mary said.

"You're really being very negative, Mary. I would *not* want to be sitting next to you on a flight to Australia." She filled her pockets with cookies and headed into the garden to climb the dogwood tree.

Sitting on the branch outside her bedroom window, she thought about Adam and Eve being banished from the Garden of Eden, and after that, cherubim and fiery swords guarding the entrance so that people in the future could not achieve immortality. Instead, the Torah became the tree of life.

Pavel had told her that if you were holding a sapling in your hand and the Messiah arrives, you must go out and plant the sapling before greeting the Messiah. The Talmudic scholars taught that trees were more important than human dreamings and longings.

She jumped down out of the tree and went inside to apologize to Mary.

* *

"Frieda, I have something to tell you," Al said one day when she came in from the gym. He had only the vaguest idea of what he wanted to say.

"Sit down," she said. "I'll get us some tea. I think I may have something to tell you, too."

He sank down into the mauve and cocoa pillows of their giant couch in the living room, imagining himself being slowly drawn inside it, like a clam sliding into a moon shell, vanishing into a long iridescent canal and then into a bulbous violet whorl, hiding inside its vermilion protuberances and pearly, puckered ribs, refusing to come out when she returned, calm and rosy-faced and plump, with her clattering tray of tea.

She placed the cups on the coffee table and poured the tea from a powder-blue porcelain pot. Sipping her tea, she sat up a little straighter. Al was staring at a glass bird. He looked over at her. She leaned toward him, poised on the edge of the couch, a woman with the same auburn curls, the same brown eyes, the same curly eyelashes as his Frieda. But it was not her.

"I had an affair once," she said. "Now I wish I had told you at the time. I'm sorry, Al."

"You had a what?" he said.

"An affair. A brief one. At a hotel." Frieda stared at him. He gazed back at her.

"A brief affair? At a hotel?" he said with a disembodied voice that did not sound like his own. "With whom?"

"Frankly, I'd rather not say. It was eight years ago. I didn't suspect it at the time, but now I think it caused the fault-line in our marriage. Daniel always says honesty is the best policy."

"But that's such a cliché," he said. "What does Daniel know about marriage? What kind of fault-line?"

"Marriages can't endure secrets."

"You're kidding, right?" he said and he laughed.

"Actually, I'm *not* kidding. It was in the afternoon. I was working weekends then, at Lenox Hill Hospital. Remember?"

He did *not* remember. "You mean, you mean you...at a hotel?" he said, but the words drifted away from him, silky and incomprehensible.

"I confessed it at the time, and I felt forgiven."

"You confessed it? To whom?"

"Father O'Flaherty."

"You didn't tell *me*, but you told a priest?"

"Yes."

"How *many* afternoons?"

"Not that many," she said.

"And were your not-that-many-afternoons enjoyable?"

"They weren't worth it, if that's what you mean."

"That's not what I mean. I mean, were they pleasurable?"

"I didn't enjoy committing a mortal sin, and I didn't enjoy deceiving you. I guess it's part of marriage but—"

"What's part of marriage?" he said.

"These tiny deceptions. Maybe it's a mistake to bring it up. It was so long ago. I'm *very* sorry, Al. But now I have a feeling we have bigger fish to fry."

"Fish don't come any bigger than secret affairs at hotels in the afternoon," he said. "Eight years ago? We hadn't been married very long. You hardly gave me a chance. Was it in the spring?"

"Yes."

"Before the daffodils, or after?"

"I don't remember," she said.

"How can you not remember? Did you have spring fever or something?"

His grandmother had always said, "Tell it not in Gath," and he and Frieda seemed to live by such rules. *Do not speak. Act it out.* He heard a plaintive call outside the window. *Ooah, cooo, cooo, coo, ooah, cooo, cooo, coo.* The hollow mournful song of a wild dove.

III

Good heavens! Mr. K., my GUIDANCE counselor, is now following Frieda's boyfriend through the streets! Waiting outside the nursing home, then sneaking behind him all the way to East 109th Street. Mr. K. is insane with jealousy, and I can identify since I am somewhat jealous of Mrs. Orzagh — Pavel's true love — but I can't imagine following her around. I have sensed for a while that Mr. K. is losing his grip on reality, and I'm afraid he may also lose his job or maybe even shoot this poor social worker who, I'm sure, is not even remotely interested in Frieda. (My journal has gotten quite spicy since I enrolled at St. Ursula's.) I believe Mr. K. has mental health issues since he grew up in a boarding house and was bounced from his mother to his grandmother, and it doesn't sound like either of them wanted him. He and Frieda don't seem to have much fun together, and I believe his biggest thrill in life is drinking chocolate martinis. It is obvious that, like me, he feels quite inadequate. His father absconded early in his life (like ten minutes after he was conceived) and he doesn't seem to have any friends. His dead grandmother sounds several sandwiches short of a picnic, and his mother was mostly interested in trying to achieve her highest aspiration: appearing in a game show on television. Oh, how ruinous to grow up in a boarding house! I force Mr. K. to talk about it, and through our discussions, I'm hoping he can purge himself of the toxins of his childhood. I can imagine the rooms where he lived smelling like Lysol and liver frying with okra, and I picture Mrs. Cobelle as this massive flowered albatross hanging around poor Al's neck and dragging him down into dank unpopularity and lifelong lack of confidence. (All you need is confidence, Vikey used to say. That trait alone will furnish the rest.) Inebriated, checked-out mother, absent father, fluffheaded grandmother, parenting provided by a houseful of lonely boarders. Not only didn't he have a goldfish or a cat or a dog, but every Sunday Mrs. Cobelle went out back and chopped the head off a chicken and made Al pluck out its feathers. And what was his destiny? To be taken into state custody when he was fourteen and get plomped onto his grandmother's farm so he could listen to her rattle her rosary beads. Then he worked his way through college and grad school, commuted on the train, lived with his grandmother, and slaved away in a hardware store near the farm, in the little village of Cold Spring. He only applied for the job at St. Ursula's because three days after his grandmother died, he met Frieda, and she goaded him into applying for a better job. So he marries Frieda, plops down in the desk chair at St. Ursula's, and doesn't move a muscle for fourteen years. Then he meets me, and we try to resurrect each other, which is like Klaus Barbie and Rudolf Hess having a picnic on the town square in Berlin. I was

depressed about nuclear weapons, and he was depressed
about Frieda. Now I'm depressed about Frieda, and he's
depressed about nuclear weapons. Oh well: Not every truth
can be blown on a trumpet.

* *

Al found Frieda's letter, which she had propped up against his bottle of Scotch, but he could only read the first two sentences of it: *It's been a long time since we've been a real couple. It wasn't just the sex—*He threw the letter into the wastebasket and poured himself a Scotch. She was gone. He had managed to stay married for fourteen years, two months, and nineteen days, and now it was official. He was a bachelor, a single man, a lone wolf.

He didn't sleep that night but lay in their king-sized bed, listening to the rain on the glass, looking at Frieda's drooping gauze curtains trimmed with satin bows. He wished he could rip the curtains down and draw them into the bed with him, into a great fuzzy soft ball in his arms.

At dawn, he got out of bed and walked into Frieda's closet. She had not packed her pastel sweat suits, but she had taken her black satin cocktail dress. He sat down on the floor, closed the door, and smelled the faint scent of marigold oil she wore when she went biking with Daniel. A male had to announce that he was available, that he owned important territory, that he was ready to fight off tres-passers, that he would cooperate with any sufficiently submissive female. Was Frieda sufficiently submissive? Was Al ready to fight off trespassers? Butterfly fish were faithful. Swans were faithful. Parrots were faithful. But could fidelity be expected of human beings?

The gold seam of light under the door reminded him of the many hours he had spent sitting on the floor of the closet at Mrs. Cobelle's, waiting for his mother to come home. He got up, put on the dreadful maroon bathrobe Frieda's mother had given him for their first Christmas, and went into the kitchen. He pulled down the shades. He couldn't bear to look over at the Rassabys' withering garden. He knew he could not go to work. He had no energy for his students, and the thought of Raine picking up on his mood and trying to wrest the truth out of him made him want to avoid all encounters with her. He felt like dumping his belongings into a huge plastic bag, joining the street people on a bench up on Broadway, and skipping all the steps in between.

In a blur of slowly falling leaves, he crossed Central Park, walked down Madison Avenue to Grand Central Station, and got on the train for Poughkeepsie. He searched the faces of the men seated around him, reading their newspapers. He wanted to turn to the man nearest him and say, "My wife left me, over the weekend, with no warning—not even a goodbye." But he said nothing, and when he got off the train in Cold Spring and looked at the herring gulls circling the river, he knew he was not ready to face the empty farmhouse.

He walked up Main Street past the pet shop, the doughnut shop, the dry cleaners, and the Chickenbone Cafe, and stopped in front of the Dooley Brothers Hardware Store. He turned the old glass doorknob and entered the store, breathing in the oily, metallic smell of hardware. The aisles were cluttered with snow shovels and bags of rock salt. He longed for the raw, bleak days of winter—a time of more sleep, more darkness, more silence. Nights longer than days, the goldfinch turning olive green, animals hiding, conserving, starving. He could feel the northern hemisphere arcing away from the sun, and creatures using all their ingenuity to survive. And he, like innumerable seeds and insect eggs, would be one more mammal drifting through winter, hoping for luck.

In his mind, he heard Frieda and Daniel reading the Bible together before their morning shift, their melodious voices blending together into a sound that had never before been heard in the universe. He felt the tears rising in his eyes, and he reached for a can of artificial snow. He wanted to go to the back of the store and find the Dooley brothers, throw his arms around them, and tell them how good they had been to him, but instead he found himself reading the small print on the can, then turning toward the door.

Walking up the hill to the farm, he stopped in the overgrown cemetery where his grandparents, his great-grandparents, and his great-great-grandparents were buried. He imagined they'd be full of accusations. Why hadn't he stayed married? Didn't his vows mean anything to him? He put one hand on the family headstone, but he couldn't think of one thing to say to these stoic farm people.

He and Frieda were married in 1984, and he barely remembered the ceremony. Had they promised to love each other "until death do us part"? He wasn't sure, and he did not think it would be prudent to ask Frieda. But why was it so important? When Frieda's patients were born, the life expectancy had been fifty; now it was nearly eighty. What was wrong with accompanying each other through fourteen fairly contented years? Why did the finish line have to be death?

He walked into the little church at the edge of the cemetery, where he had spent so much time with his grandmother. The sanctuary was empty, but he could still see the women kneeling in their flowered scarves. The church smelled of damp wool, mold, must, and incense, and he could almost hear the groggy voice of the priest intoning his prayers.

He and his grandmother had sat in the third pew, where he fidgeted with her blue glass rosary beads as she prayed. Sometimes he closed his eyes and ran his fingers over the silky cord of the scapular around her neck. When he went with her up to the communion rail, he could see the reflection of the priest's vestments swaying in the wine.

He walked out of the church and up the hill a half mile to the farmhouse, which was built into the side of the hill, tipping slightly toward the ravine. It stood in a pasture beside a lopsided barn. He followed the red dirt lane down through the pasture and stepped up onto the old porch. Wild grapevines hung down off the rafters. The windows were covered with spiderwebs.

Al and his grandmother had loved early spring when the skunk cabbage bloomed, polka-dotted salamanders hid under rocks, jelly-clouds of frogs' eggs floated in the pond, puddles filled up with transparent fairy shrimp, swimming on their backs, propelling themselves forward with their leaflike legs. They loved the chickadees singing their courting songs and the butterflies with blue spots and velvet-brown wings.

His mother drank too much ginger ale, his grandmother had told him. It was a foolish statement, yet one she stood by as long as she lived. Though Al had tried, he had never been able to talk to her about the alcohol. He and his grandmother seemed to know that words could never be as true as other ways of knowing, but something between them *was* true, and it was the warmest and safest feeling he had ever known.

* *

Raine dropped a dead bird on Al's desk—a gray siskin with a flash of yellow on its tail.

"Look at this poor bird," she said.

Al hated the sight of the bird lying on his messy desk. He imagined it singing with a coarse and wheezy whistle. "You brought a dead animal into my office?" he said.

"I felt sorry for it. I couldn't leave it in the street."

"I don't want dead birds in here. Do you mind?"

"You can't hide from death, Mr. K."

"I'm not trying to hide from death. I'm asking you *not* to bring dead birds into my office."

He looked down at the bird's bent ribs, its mysterious, opaque eye—an animal struck down by some quirk of nature, a creature made to be beautiful, to sing.

"I'm planning a funeral for it," she said. "In my garden. Would you like to come?"

She reached across the desk and placed her hand on his arm. Long, pale fingers. Piano fingers. She smiled at him. He froze. His arm began to tingle, though her hand was barely touching his sleeve. He declined the invitation, moving away from her and glancing across the desk at her tangled loops of hair, the odd way her eyes were changing color from violet to purple and back to gray. He looked in her eyes and saw a vast expanse—restful, wise—an oasis of lavender.

She picked up the bird and the door snapped closed

behind her. Al's head began to buzz. He grabbed his coat and hurried up the stairs and through the castle-like doors of the school, down the steps, and out onto Riverside Drive. He crossed the street and walked through the park, the trees and river gliding past him in a blur of shadow and light. The Hudson shone at his side, a brackish scarlet, darkly rippling.

He turned the corner, wishing he could return to the day as it had been that morning. Two months had passed since the first time he had talked to Raine Rassaby in her garden, and now he felt himself being drawn into her life. He sank down on a bench and listened to a sparrow singing. His grandmother had taught him that song sparrows sang nine hours a day, ridding themselves of their nervous energy. Songs helped birds locate one another. Birds sometimes sang until they found a mate, then fell silent. Song warned of danger and helped to simplify the complex rituals of breeding life.

He thought of Frieda in her hot pink and turquoise fluorescent biking clothes. How odd it was that women often dressed in bright colors, wore jewelry and perfume, and curled and colored their hair for the drab male, following the example of polyandrous females. Women were not compelled to follow their biological destiny; instead, language permitted them to be motivated by a combination of biology and culture. Yet here Frieda was, becoming immersed in the reproductive strategies of her species. Or had some other compulsion lured her away from him?

Now he was free, but free to do what? Dream up fantasies for himself, as his mother and the boarders at Mrs. Cobelle's had done? The flowers in Raine's garden were golden and wilted, but he found himself envisioning the soil overgrown with summer flowers and himself surrounded by Mrs. Rassaby playing the violin, Mary rolling out piecrusts, Mr. Rassaby looking through his telescope, and Raine smiling appreciatively down at him from the branches of the tree.

He now ate his meals in a coffee shop. He liked the New York City waiters and waitresses treating him impersonally. In Cold Spring, they would have been inquiring, wondering where Frieda had gone, asking how he was doing. The waiters' lack of curiosity was a comfort, allowing him to rest inside his secret. He still wore his wedding ring, and sometimes he took it off and studied the inscription carved into the gold: *F.M.F. 8-15-84*.

He did not want to sleep with Raine. He wasn't sure he even wanted to talk to her, although he loved the honesty that sometimes sprang up between them. He wanted to tell her about Frieda being gone. What would she say? He wanted to tell her about Frieda's affair. He wished he could have a small but secure and circumspect place in her life. Couldn't they spend time together in her garden?

Couldn't she lie in the hammock singing her doleful songs as he sat beside her, feeling the well of joy that waits for all creatures beneath the scars and terrors of life?

He walked through the streets bordering Riverside Park. What he would give Raine was not his presence but his distance. He must listen for her, he must make her feel the power of his devotion. He was a medieval man, adoring a forbidden lady. She would love the adoration. She would feel its safety.

* *

Al watched the rain dripping from the crab apples outside his window for a long time before he realized that Raine had left her books on his desk. He turned to his computer to check for the room number of her next class when he noticed a little flowered book stuck inside a copy of a magazine called *Insects Are People Too*. Lured into the small rectangle of flowers, he opened to the first page and read:

Stay Out!
The Story of My Life, Volume 18,
Beginning September 1, 1998, Ending
June 23, 1999—Graduation Day!
St. Ursula's Academy
Girl-Changing-into-Woman Territory

The journal was covered with peonies. Of course he would not read it. He piled it with her textbooks on the table in the corner and sat down at his desk, then he got up, walked across the room, and opened the door. He looked down the hallway, hoping she'd return for her books. But the hallway was empty. Jesus standing in the Garden of Gethsemane was gazing at him with syrupy gold eyes. Al checked the time. He wanted to go home and soak in the tub. He imagined taking the little flowered book and sinking with the dark scrawled words, like Houdini in his chained and padlocked trunk, to the bottom of the sea.

At three-thirty, he slammed the window shut and put on his jacket. On his way out the door, he snatched the flowered journal from the table and dropped it into the pocket of his raincoat. Walking up Riverside Drive, he envisioned the little journal in his pocket softening like a cherry pit in the stomach of a bird.

He stopped on the corner of Riverside Drive and West 88th Street. His only hope of salvaging his integrity was to walk up her street and slip the journal through the shiny brass slot of the Rassabys' red front door. But what if her parents found it?

At midnight, he was in his study, drinking a cup of Ovaltine, picturing Daniel Wadhams's face blurring into the face of Frieda's anonymous lover. Misty orange light shone out of the adjacent brownstone. A ship's horn was blowing. He went into their bedroom, balled up a clump of bathrobes and shirts and tucked the hump into Frieda's side of the bed. Then he pulled the covers up and returned to his den. A thin river fog was rising in the air, covering the lighted brownstones in a pale haze.

St. Ursula's Academy did not have a place for Raine, and he could not create one. What she was lacking was the desire to please. If he taught her anything it would be to pretend, to satisfy the nuns, to get a diploma that would lead her on to college. Yet in some ways he did not want to shepherd her back into the flock. She was the one who had strayed, and part of him wanted her to stray farther and even lead him on—but it was his job, his moral obligation, to beckon her back to fealty.

He remembered Raine's stories of Pavel—and he felt himself becoming entangled with her desires, with her dark Slovakian roots, with her grandmother, with Hitler, with Freud, with a world that was neatly divided into good and evil. When he closed his eyes, he could hear violins and bagpipes playing. What was happening to him? *Take what you want and pay for it,* the Spanish proverb said. He opened the flowered journal and read:

> *Al thinks I'm a one-trick pony, but I'm not exactly sure what HE knows. Still, he's cute—especially in his white shirt, his paisley tie, and his navy-blue herringbone vest. But I know it's only because I'm so bored and dissatisfied with myself that I have to pick on teachers for my icons of interest.*

Even though I'm influenced by the world around me, I'm trying to keep myself as sacred as possible. At school, I'm usually trying my best not to be noticed for being different at the same time I want to be seen and appreciated for who I really am. I just wish I could find someone I can talk to who isn't getting paid to listen to me. When Mother isn't on tour, she's practicing, then she lies in her bed wearing black velvet eye pads stuffed with flaxseeds, with the blinds pulled down, as Mary paints her toenails red and I walk in circles around her bed, talking. I don't believe she listens to me, though. I remember when she went on concert tours to Europe, how awful I'd feel, and Mary and I would put one flower in the vase on the table every morning, and when the vase was full, it would be time for her to come home. I loved coming down every morning and seeing another flower in the vase. Then one day, a taxi pulled up, and I'd run down the steps and get all tangled up in Mother's perfume and scarves and fur. She'd kiss me and give me a little package. It was always wrapped in tissue paper and I loved the way it crinkled as I held it in my hand. She'd laugh and say, "Open it, darling!" (She almost never calls me darling.) So I would, reluctantly, because it was the best feeling just holding her gift in my hand, with Mary standing on the steps, smiling at us. Once the gift was a little glass fish filled with cologne. Once it was a Roumanian book with a green satin bookmark. Once it was a

Scottish flute. Once it was a tiny samovar. Then Mary cooked Mother's favorite dinner, Peking duck. I always felt sorry for the duck, but it was fun to sit there, watching Mother eat it. On those nights, she seemed happy to have me as a daughter. The next day, I expected her to pay a lot of attention to me—the way she had the night before, but she never did.

I love going to her concerts and watching her with bands of silver sparkling in her hair and the lights shining down on the rich burnt gold of her violin that was once a tree, a violin that knows all her secrets like the pink dogwood in the garden knows all my secrets. I sit there like someone sitting before a shrine. When the concert ends, I hug her and hold my face against her and her arms are always filled with bouquets and people are reaching out for her. But then I get nudged out of the way. For me, watching Mother is almost a form of worship—healthy or unhealthy, I don't know— but centering and elating like worship always is.

———

I think it's nice that Mrs. Orzagh throws potatoes when she gets mad, because everyone in my house is always expressing their stupid opinions but no one ever expresses their feelings.

I told Dr. Hadcock that sometimes I feel like a clump of cells that just arranged themselves into a girl for no particular reason, and after that, she asked me to participate in a study of eccentrics. She said it was unusual for women as young as me to become eccentric, since women are taught to be attractive, docile, and helpful, and they wait until later in life to climb out on limbs. I informed her that in my opinion, it's the world that's eccentric, not me. She said that eccentricity isn't something to be embarrassed about and that eccentrics are actually happier than most people because they don't care what other people think.

Dr. Hadcock has these glorious intelligent eyes which seem to know everything yet miss an awful lot. Sometimes I feel very soothed by her, but other times I feel like yelling, "Stop talking so much—you get paid to listen. Freud never said one word!"

This is our conversation about Pavel:

She: When you think about him, what do you think?

Me: I want to be with him.

She: And do what?

Me: Just be with him and listen to him playing the cello and singing in my ear.

LONG PAUSE

She: Perhaps you love Pavel and there is no cure for love.

For this kind of cheesy dialogue, she gets paid a hundred and thirty dollars an hour!

———

Not one menorah or prayer book or mezuzah in our house. Except in my room. If Mrs. Orzagh ever drops in for scones, she'll be apoplectic.

———

Sometimes I bury my face in a rose after the sun's been shining on it all day, and I look at it and see all the soft veins in it and the way the color lightens a little and the petals curl at the edges. I hold it up to the sun and look at the milky veins in the leaves. Then I think if we have a war, if someone drops too many bombs, there'll never be another rose.

———

The church used to hold us to impossible ideals, and now I feel that the impossible ideals are supplied by the media. Well, that's the way it is, I guess, just like the old Tarzan movies, sometimes the alligator's on top and sometimes Tarzan is.

———

I sit in class dreaming of Pavel creeping up to my room at night. I picture him on the stairs like Eros tiptoeing up to Psyche, and me jumping up and throwing my stuffed animal collection in the closet and lighting some incense, and him crawling into my bed. If he came up to my room at night what he'd come for is my soul. It would feel splendid to him, like a moon in the bed. He would find it irresistible—something that's deep and calm and true, the thing that makes me unique in the universe. What I picture with Pavel is not exactly sex but something else that's exquisite that I have to have more of—I don't know exactly what. But we would both be wearing the mask of our real selves.

* *

It scared him, the way Raine came into his office, pounded on his desk and said, "I am *not* a bird so you can quit looking at me through your binoculars!"

He looked up. "No, you're not a bird. You're a girl."

"I am *not* a girl. I'm a woman. One who does not appreciate being observed through selfish circles of glass—and I doubt very much if the birds do either."

She slammed the door and was gone. He leaned back in his chair, wishing he had a lock on his office door. He had read somewhere that a kneeling coward can't know what a fall is. Spooling downward, spooling downward...he could feel himself falling. He was trying to stay perpendicular to the world, to break his own fall, but he could feel the universe slowing down, slackening, the wondrous mixtures of gases upon which life so frailly rested creating a vacuum of hydrogen, carbon monoxide, ammonia and methane. Could one rise above the disorder to discern patterns where there only seemed to be chaos? He never drank Scotch anymore. But his abstinence made him feel more vulnerable because now, when he seemed to be wandering through a fog, there was no bottle he could forswear, no glass he could put down.

Raine seemed almost angelic, and he awoke to her smiles, he fell asleep to her frowns. All day long, he recited wise things to her in his head, yet when she appeared in his office twice a week, he said very little, imagining himself turning into a pillar of salt, as his grandmother had predicted. An affair in a hotel in the afternoon was a sin, yet it had probably involved joy and transcendence and indelible fragrances and inferences of immortality, whereas his fascination with a schoolgirl furnished only netherworlds of anguish and the merest shreds of joy.

Walking through the streets, he longed for a simpler time. He wished he were back on the farm. Perhaps he and his grandmother had not been happy, but at least it had been a time of innocence. The rising sun, the setting sun, the changing moon, the corn knee-high by the fourth of July, the village church bells calling worshippers to Mass.

He remembered his days as an altar boy, the priest raising his hand, Alvin slipping the cruet into it, the priest dropping his eyelids, Alvin ringing the golden bells. He tried to retain these images of himself as a normal person, but he was falling fast, as sure of his destination as a spider on a web. Did the spider feel terrified of the fall, or thrilled by it? If only Raine had not brought that siskin into his office and forced him to feel sorry for it. Had the bird somehow ignited his insistent need to rescue her, to keep her safe?

Medieval gardens were calling to him with their orderly boxed shrubs, their laurel and bay and yew, their wattle fences and hedges of roses, their primroses and wild marigolds and oxtongue and henbane, white lilies and wild teasel—a cloistered sanctuary where one could be accosted by death, by a visitation from the Blessed Virgin, or by peace. Oh, mulberries! Oh, flowery mede! Oh, bee-garden! Oh love!

* *

He wandered one evening into a lingerie store on Amsterdam Avenue, a shop called Le Petit Magasin. He had never been a man to spend money. People who don't spend emotion have trouble spending money, Frieda had informed him during one of their fights. But it was not an actual fight, since he and Frieda rarely fought. Instead they stifled their feelings, then bickered, then stifled their feelings again. They rarely emerged from conflict with a deeper understanding of each other.

He went into Le Petit Magasin and came out with a plum-colored lace slip as a gift for Frieda in his pocket. The slip, had he paid for it, would have cost him eighty-three dollars. He liked reaching into the pocket of his sport jacket and touching the soft lace.

He went to Gristede's to shop for the ingredients to cook Frieda's favorite meal, trying to remember the menu she had requested. He found some mushrooms and broccoli rabe and thought he remembered some kind of chicken. The cake had a strange name. He settled for a box of chocolate cake mix, then put it back, remembering that chocolate was his favorite, not hers. Instead he chose lemon—his second favorite—then put it back and picked up a yellow cake mix with a tub of chocolate icing. He circled around the store, picking up more things: Portuguese cooking sherry, watermelon rind, pineapple salsa, portobello marinara sauce, French mustard, lemon curd. He deliberated over each item. Again and again, he went up and down the same aisles in the same order, feeling like a drunk trying to remember what he needed, then remembering, then forgetting again.

At the root of his agitation was his awareness that he needed nothing at the supermarket because he did not have a wife. The thought struck him suddenly, as though he had half-known it before but was only now realizing that Frieda was gone. Hurriedly, he placed more items in his cart: smoked salmon and black caviar and canned Arctic char and Assam tea and soft gray capers gleaming in glass.

People streamed past him. He had always done the grocery shopping, but he could not now shop and cook for her because it was too late. Still he kept circling, piling the cart with things he thought she might like—horseradish sauce, black beluga lentils, organic mesclun, Ghirardelli chocolate. The fluorescent lights were flickering; the store was about to close. He wheeled the cart past the cashiers and out through the automatic door onto the sidewalk.

Then he stopped and wondered what to do. He heard voices. A security guard in a blue uniform placed a hand on his arm. Al looked into the man's wrinkled face, as though he were looking into the mirror thirty years from now. He found no kindness there, no glimmerings of warmth, no interest whatsoever in Al's plight. The guard could not be made to care that Al had been a faithful Gristede's customer for fourteen years. The face was so familiar—so known to him—the cold brown eyes, the fishy smile, the gleer of self-concern. He wondered if the man could be his father.

It was all a misunderstanding that could easily be cleared up, he was sure. He was no thief. One telephone call to the bank would confirm that he had plenty of money in his checking account. This shopping trip—this night—was merely some sort of departure. Nature veered off at times—sometimes wildly—before returning to its course. Who knew why? If he had been hit by a bag of sand falling from a roof, no one would arrest him for it, yet that was more or less what had happened to him in Gristede's. He felt sure that the police could be made to understand his lapse even if this security guard could not.

He had not really stolen the groceries. He had merely stepped outside the supermarket with them. He had simply not been paying attention. But when the police arrived, they searched him, found the woman's slip in his pocket, and asked him for the receipt.

Then fear struck him. Perhaps the police would not be sympathetic to such an ordinary tale of betrayal. Of course he was not a thief, but they could not know him as he knew himself, and who was there to stand up for him? Frieda could not be counted on, and he had not heard from anyone in their meager group of friends since she left him. He had a few college friends, but he had not seen them in years, and they might recall what a loner he had been, even then. He had spent his life trying not to be noticed—and now a crowd of people, gathered on the sidewalk, was staring at him. He felt that he was part of an old movie as he rolled in the police car through the streets he knew so well—his own neighborhood—with his hands clasped in handcuffs.

As the police car crept along, he thought of the farm with its thickets of wild roses, its trails of lupine and day lilies, its scarlet clematis climbing up over the milk house, its juniper shrubs covered with pale blue berries. He wondered if it was really the birds in Raine's garden he was interested in when he picked up his binoculars each morning. Oh, the luxury of that garden, each bloom magnified through glass—larkspur and hollyhocks, old-fashioned flowers his grandmother had loved.

He longed to settle comfortably back into the routines of his life, however boring they may have been. He had spent his life being bashful and aloof. Playing poker once a month with a group of men who were married to Frieda's friends, he had been careful to keep himself concealed, and he had been hiding, even from himself, all those nights he had become inebriated in his den.

With a steel grate between him and the two policemen, he felt caged like an unruly German shepherd—yet the confines of the police car illuminated his life in a way that nothing else had.

* *

Al was sitting in the 25th Precinct at a table strewn with papers. On the wall was a photograph of Alfred Auster, also known as Otto Isenschmid, a fugitive wanted for first-degree murder. He pictured his own photograph displayed on the wall, and Mrs. Cobelle walking in and saying, "I knew that boy would never amount to a hill of beans."

The door opened. It was Raine. "Al," she said, walking into the room. "Let's use our heads for more than hat racks."

"Hi, Raine. It was nice of you to come."

She sat down across from him and said, "I'm glad you called me. Thank you for giving me this chance to perform a *mitzvah*."

"I didn't know who else to call," he said. "That was a terrible moment, when I realized I couldn't call Frieda, and I couldn't think of anyone else."

"How come you couldn't call Frieda?" she said.

"I was afraid to call the Mother Superior. So *you* got elected."

"Mary went to the bank to get some bail money. I don't

think Mother and Daddy will mind. All the way over here, I was wondering what you had done and hoping it wasn't anything too sleazy."

"I got arrested for stealing, Raine."

"Really?"

"Yes," he said.

"What did you steal?"

"Some groceries."

"Groceries?" she said.

"And a woman's slip."

"Oh my God—are you a cross-dresser?"

"The slip was for Frieda. I stole it from a little shop on Amsterdam Avenue. Then I went to Gristede's and bought all this food I thought she'd like. But I didn't pay for it. I just walked out of the store with a cart stacked with all this exotic stuff."

"We can give you money for groceries, Al."

"Raine, I had enough cash in my wallet to pay for the slip, and I had a credit card to pay for the groceries. The store added them up. $293 worth."

"You spent $293 on groceries?"

"I didn't spend a nickel—that's the problem. I don't know what happened. It's sad to be married to a woman for fourteen years and not even know what she likes to eat. It's pathetic. But maybe it explains why Frieda would leave me."

"Frieda left you?"

"Yes."

"Really? What was the problem?"

"There were issues it wouldn't be proper to talk to you about. Serious infractions."

"It sounds like kind of a lame crime, but as soon as Mary gets here with the money, we'll get you out of here."

"That's very kind of you and Mary, but they just came in and told me they're planning to let me go. I have to show up in court April 16. And I have to see a psychiatrist."

"I don't think Dr. Hadcock is terribly competent, but you could try her," she said.

"Thanks anyway, but it wouldn't be wise for me to use your psychiatrist."

"I'll go to court with you," she said.

"You don't need to. You've done enough. Thank you."

They sat and stared at the police sketch of the serial killer Floyd Smith.

"I feel very sorry for him," Raine said.

"Well, don't. Some people participate in their own doom."

"I'm going to Nebraska with Pavel next week," she said.

"Nebraska?"

"We're taking the bus. We're going to see a nuclear missile silo."

"It's okay with your parents?"

"My mother has a concert in Glasgow, and my dad's

spending most of the week in Washington. So what could they say?"

"Be careful, Raine."

"Did Frieda go off with that guy at work?"

"I hate to admit it," he said. "It makes it seem so real. I went up to the farm one weekend to fix the roof, and when I got back Sunday night, she had moved out. She left me a letter."

"She left you a *letter*?"

"It's interesting the way your worst fears come true if you nurture them long enough."

"Everything will turn out fine, Al. You'll see a shrink and you'll get off doing community service. I just know you will. I'm absolutely positive."

"Thanks for the pep talk, Raine. It was very enjoyable."

* *

Al has become my new pet project. He has lived the life of a dog for too long, while I have been living the life of a poodle on a leash. Yesterday, he got ARRESTED! (He seems to be following in my footsteps.) When he was a kid, his mother worked at Gimbel's selling handbags, and everyone liked her and thought she was pretty and sweet— and she was, before she picked up a whiskey bottle and had a couple of nips. I complain quite frequently about Mother, but she certainly looks quite maternal compared to Katy Alice Klepatar. Yes, I have temporarily become Al's psychi-

atrist because he absolutely refuses to make himself an appointment with Dr. Hadcock, and who does he have to talk to except me—and now, sadly—the judge? So I am forced to search for patterns in his life as a thief. You do not need a medical degree to notice that Katy Alice and Frieda have certain things in common: namely, a boyfriend problem. Why does Al choose women who do not show up for him? Okay, maybe he didn't choose his mother, but when we are trying to decipher problems, we must not be too literal. Al is reluctant to transport information to me (since I am supposedly his professional responsibility), so I must niggle it out of him as cunningly as possible. I have extracted the names of the boarders he lived with at Mrs. Cobelle's: Mr. Swazy, Charlene Onofrio, Reginald Jones, Hope Alswang, and Khawar Saeed. I have been forced to ask myself why Mr. Swazy would not come forth with his first name, and I have decided he must have been a pedophile. Now, the real question is, did he proposition Al? I simply cannot ask Al this question because he flares easily and although he does not say this, I believe the slightest mention of SEX in our conversations causes him to see himself being fired by the Mother Superior for unethical conduct with a student. Honestly, Al is afraid of everything. I do not judge him for this since I also am scared of so much. Besides, he had no father, his mother was non compos mentis, Mrs. Cobelle was an upholstered chair with a mean streak, and his grandmother was madly in love with Jesus Christ. All he ever really had were the Dooley brothers, who owned the hardware store where Al worked for years. He started working there when he was sixteen, went to college at N.Y.U., went to graduate school, graduated, and STILL worked for the Dooley brothers selling aerosol cans of horrible poisonous insecticides. The sweetest tale in the world is of the Dooley brothers themselves, who actually closed their store, put on suits and ties, and appeared at Al's high school graduation. Four years later, they took the train to the city and went to his college graduation, and two years later, they showed up again when he got his graduate degree. But was Al's grandmother there? I am afraid she wasn't, so I do not interrogate him on that subject. But I do know her name was Blanche.

I have spent the entire day on top of a huge rock in Central Park, reading Common Sense and becoming enamored of Thomas Paine. (I am now sitting in my room with frostbite of the extremities, and it is quite possible that I will be going to the hospital later to have my toes amputated.) I believe I have felt oppressed for quite a long time, but some higher thing speaks to me and after reading this book, I feel like an immigrant in a babushka sailing past the Statue of Liberty. I have never been able to figure out if America is a bunch of promises we don't intend to keep, or if it is something astonishingly beautiful that we have carried in our hearts from another land. Justice, Liberty, Freedom, Equality, Opportunity, and the Pursuit of Happiness. These are dreams. They're ideas. My generation has inherited them from our parents, who (with the exception of Raisa and Karel) smoked pot in their youth, went barefoot, ate nasturtiums, and knew how to dream but did not know how to make their dreams come true. I feel it is up to my generation to read *Common Sense* and go, Whoa, Tonto! Since when has America been about making bombs and making money? Oh, Thomas Paine, thank you! I am thrilled down to my goddess tattoo when I read your words:

O! ye that love Mankind! Ye that dare oppose not only the tyranny but the tyrant, stand forth! Every spot of the Old World is overrun with oppression. Freedom hath been hunted round the globe. Asia and Africa have long expelled her. Europe regards her like a stranger and England hath given her warning to depart.

O! receive the fugitive and prepare in time an asylum for mankind.

* *

Raine sat in the Pig 'N Pancake in Sunflower City, Nebraska, and wondered what it would be like to be from such a small town. Maybe it would be like being a member of a tribe, like being from Banska Stiavnica, knowing who you were and what people expected of you. The people in the restaurant looked content, as though they were living far from the shadow of a nuclear missile silo. They were floating in a cloud of illusions—but everyone said she was, too. She was fooling herself that Pavel loved her, wasn't she? She looked around at the signs saying *Do Not Sit at a Dirty Table,* and the words blurred, the letters rearranged themselves until they said *Pavel Is Going to Dump You.* She turned to the woman sitting next to her at the counter and said, "Do you like living here?"

"Yes I do, dear," the woman said, reaching for Raine's hand. "My name is Violet Wells."

"Do you come here every morning?"

"Oh no. I have a rule. Bacon and eggs once a week."

"I'm Raine Rassaby. I'm in town with my boyfriend. He's off in the woods, shokeling."

"Is that one of those new sports?" Violet Wells said.

"No—it's old. It's Jewish for sort of rocking back and forth while you pray. He's an old Jew, and I'm a new Jew. My whole family were Christians who left Slovakia a few years after Hitler invaded. My boyfriend and I came to Nebraska to see a missile silo. So we could hate and despise it in person."

Violet Wells did not respond. Raine sat listening to the man sitting at the counter on her other side. "When I got married, I never had a clean shirt," he said to the waitress, "and I tried to explain to my wife that I needed a new shirt every day, and it had to be ironed. My mother always

wrapped my father's shirts up and put them in the refriger-
ator and the moisture made them easier to iron, so when I
got married, I just assumed—"

Raine sat and studied the menu. Dungeness Crab
Scramble. Dreaming of Mexico Stew. At the top of the
menu were the words: "IS IT REALLY MORNING?"

She tapped the man on the shoulder and said, "Don't
assume things—iron them yourself!"

* *

Nebraska was full of fields of dead sunflowers and
ancient sand dunes covered with prairie grass. Pavel
claimed it was a biblical place, prone to invasions of
grasshoppers.

On the bus home, Raine said, "Are you really attracted
to me, Pavel?"

"What do you mean?"

"I mean, do you desire me?"

"Sure. Of course. Sometimes I do."

"When don't you?" she said.

"Is this another one of your in-depth interrogations?"

"I was just wondering how you feel. What about last
night?"

"What about it?"

"Did you have fun?" she said.

"Yeah. Did you?"

"I guess so."

"What do you mean?" he said.

"Just that there's so much talk about how fabulous sex is. But for me, the best part was afterward, lying there and talking to you and feeling this wall that's sometimes between us sort of collapse. You were really warm, Pavel."

"Thank you."

"Which you're not always," she said.

"What do you mean by that?"

"I don't always know how you're going to be. Sometimes you act like you're wild about me, and sometimes you're cold as the north side of a gravestone. Maybe because of Mother Influence."

"Women analyze everything. Men don't like to talk about things that aren't rational and logical."

"Like love?"

"Like ambivalence."

"So you feel ambivalent about me?" she said.

"I guess so. I don't mean to hurt your feelings, but it's just that sometimes you're so intense, Raine."

"That's not what you said last night. Or maybe it was the night before. You said I'm the only woman you ever loved."

"That's love-talk," he said.

"Lies, you mean?"

"No, not lies."

"But don't you think love and truth have to go together?" she said.

"People have sex all the time, and they think it's fun, but it happens to be something I feel confused about, I guess because I'm not very trusting. It's very hard to take your clothes off and get in bed and announce to another person that you're open to bodily explorations."

"Bodily explorations?" she said. "Isn't it more like expressing your deepest emotions?"

"But all of that's only words. You should just feel what you feel without getting embroiled in conversations that completely miss the point."

"What *is* the point?"

"The point of what?" he said.

"Of sleeping together."

"Talking about it ruins everything."

They were in the Badlands, and she could picture burning coal mines, lonely mammal bones, bands of coal, and terrible blue plants with fangs growing up out of the black hills, as screeching animals with yellow teeth ran through petrified forests.

"There's something I want to tell you," he said. "I've decided to become a rabbi. I'm leaving for rabbinical school at the end of March. That's why I'm saving my money."

"You're kidding," she said.

"No. I'm going to Ohr Torah Stone."

"What's that?"

"It's in Israel, Raine."

"In *Israel*? Wow." She closed her eyes and pictured him with a long beard and a black hat, standing by the Wailing Wall in Jerusalem. "Was being a rabbi your mother's idea?"

"No," he said. "I've always wanted to be a rabbi."

She had never been able to imagine her life without Pavel. It never occurred to her that he might become a rabbi, or anything else for that matter. It never occurred to her that he might leave New York. It seemed that they'd always be together, and nothing unusual would ever happen to them, and even if they got arrested for damaging a nuclear weapon—and she hoped they would—they'd sit together in court, holding hands, and write each other long love letters from prison.

"I thought we were going to get rid of nuclear weapons," she said.

"We will."

"When?"

"When I get out of school."

"How long will that take?"

"Six years."

"Six years! What about all the nuclear weapons that are on hair-trigger alert? Are you just going to be apathetic like everyone else?"

"Apathetic? Rabbis spend their lives grappling with the deepest issues of life."

"But I thought you said St. Ursula's Girls Against the

Atomic Bomb was going to get bigger and bigger and bigger. Remember how Gandhi said our faith in God has to be equal to our confidence in our own efforts?"

"I believe that," he said.

"But if we're all just working on our *careers*...."

"Being a rabbi is a professional vocation. When you get called to do a great thing, you have to respond."

"Remember how cold your mother was to me at the picnics?" she said.

"She found out you go to Catholic school."

"Why does that matter?"

"Judaism is her whole life, and it's getting watered down. Jews have to defend against it. If we don't, there won't be anything left of us."

"Did you tell her about the Seders we had up in my room?"

"No. She thinks people should have Seders on Passover."

"Did you tell her my grandmother hid Jews in her potato cellar?"

"No—but your grandmother told her, at one of the picnics, and she didn't like that either. She doesn't think people should advertise their *mitzvahs*."

"Maybe you could tell her Vikey knew Freud, since he was the most famous Jew of all time."

"My mother doesn't like Freud. She thinks he was an

egomaniac. He didn't believe in God. He abandoned his religion."

"What do you mean? The Nazis almost killed him for being a Jew."

"Well, that's her opinion."

"When we get home, do you still want me to come over for dinner?"

"Sure."

"I'll tell your mother I'm planning to keep a kosher kitchen when I settle down."

"Raine," he said, laughing. "She knows Mary cooks all your meals, and you wouldn't know how to defer to a man if your life depended on it."

"I defer to you. We always do things your way. You don't even realize it, Pavel. It's the patriarchy at its quietest."

"A lot of stuff between men and women is complicated."

"So you mean sometimes you're attracted to me and sometimes you're not?"

"I mean I'm a Jew, and things aren't easy for us."

"I'm a Jew, too," she said.

"You play at being a Jew. You romanticize the experience. It isn't that you're phony or anything. No one's less phony than you are. But you're still three-quarters Catholic. And your grandmother was a convert. She wasn't floundering under the burden of thousands of years of suspicion and hatred. We'll never see things through the same eyes, Raine."

"Why do we have to?"

"We don't. But we'll never be one the way a Jewish couple is supposed to be. It's just a matter of ancient antipathies."

"You didn't say anything about ancient antipathies last night," she said.

"We weren't talking last night. You were the one who wanted to put all this into words. Remember?"

* *

Raine flopped down on top of her duffel bag in the kitchen and groaned. Mary was mixing a pot of chocolate pudding on the stove with a wooden spoon.

"It was a long trip," Mary said. "I looked at the map."

"I know. I thought Nebraska was next to Ohio, but it wasn't."

"Did you have fun?"

"Actually, it was fantastic," Raine said. "Guess what, Mary? We had sex."

Mary put down her spoon and smiled.

"It wasn't exactly like it looks in the movies. Sex has always been pretty confusing to me. All the magazines and movies make it seem like it's about the way you look, the way you wear your hair. It's not about what's inside you. It's not about what you feel. Then there's the church, telling me I have to get married and I'll burn in hell for it if I don't. And my father thinking, 'Pet your dog, not your date.' And that billboard up on Broadway saying, 'A tisket a tasket, a condom or a casket.'"

"So it was good?" Mary said.

"Pavel's a little shy. He's always been very, very unaggressive. At the picnics, I used to wear shorts and a T-shirt because if I wore a sundress, I knew he'd try to avoid me. He wasn't really ready for a woman."

"So he was a boy, and now he's a man," Mary said.

"We were planning to sleep on the bus all week, but I had Mother's credit card, so we spent three nights at the Ho-Hum Motel in Sunflower City, Nebraska. That's when we saw the missile silo, so it was this really weird mixture of eros and thanatos."

"I hope you protected yourselves," Mary said.

"We did. Pavel had a bunch of condoms. Every time he leaves the house, his mother says, 'Don't forget your umbrella.' He said he loved me, but then he took it back. He's planning to become a rabbi. I wish he had told me sooner."

"Being a rabbi will be a good profession," Mary said.

"I *cannot* picture myself sharing Pavel with a whole synagogue full of Jews." She put her arms around Mary and said, "So are you ready to tell me if you're in love with Mr. Jezuliana?"

"Only white people fall in love," Mary said. She poured the pudding into glass bowls and Raine licked the spoon. Then she dragged her duffel bag up to her room, lay in her bed with her feet on the wall, and wrote:

> A visit to the nuclear missile silo planted in a field in Sunflower City, Nebraska, brought forth the sight of this fence marked with a No Trespassing sign, and inside it was this slab of concrete and a few steel poles. Pavel told me about the Hopi women who soothe their children when they fall down and then smooth out the wound in the earth that was caused by the fall. While I was looking at this monstrosity, I started thinking about the cement-pourers, the fence-makers, the backhoe guys, the people working in the missile factories, and I realized that none of them participated in building that missile silo out of hatred. All of them were working for money. I tried to picture the cars and houses the workers had bought with the money. I thought of how much better it would have been if the guy sitting inside the silo in his Air Force uniform really felt something about what he was doing, if he really hated everyone and everything he was willing to destroy. But I figured he was probably just sitting there bored, not thinking about much, looking at his watch. I wondered who along the chain from senator to taxpayer to weapons designer to factory worker to truck driver to guard felt anything about that missile silo. But then I tried to calm myself down by remembering that

humans once made weapons out of stones and bones and antlers and later abandoned them, so we could abandon the missile silos, too. I told myself that life is always creeping from lower to higher forms. The world was too dangerous for reptiles—so they became mammals who were smarter and could adapt and protect their young by keeping them inside their bodies and by making their own food. So now we're living in a time when in order to survive we have to make another leap, and I guess we're lucky because we aren't stuck with instinct. We can invent new behavior.

———

It is now December 15. Pavel comes over less and less often, and he has not come forth with the invitation to dinner that he alluded to on the bus, but Janey says I should dump him and work on my own life. She met him one day at the Central Park Zoo when he ambled up to us wearing a Russian fur hat and smoking a cigar, and she says he has a streak of cruelty. It's funny I never noticed that, but she swears it's true. Janey is extremely smart. She plans to start a chapter of St. Ursula's Girls Against the Atomic Bomb at Princeton, and I made her swear she won't rename the group, but I guess it doesn't matter if she does.

The biggest story of this journal opens not in Verona, Italy, but at the Ho-Hum Motel in Sunflower City, Nebraska, with Ms. Raine Marie Rassaby, notorious for her anti-nuclear zeal, and Mr. Pavel Orzagh, known for his fiery oratory. Who would have ever thought that this was the epic setting where they would have their first serious passionate encounter? Cinderblock walls, orange bedspread, trains going by and rattling the velvet paintings on the walls. Pavel was sweet and considerate in bed, which was somewhat surprising to our heroine. The fantasy and the reality are often quite at odds, but the great thing is that the reality was really nice. In our queen-sized bed, the whole world went away, which I guess is what intimacy is. Sister Claudette said that when she was in high school during the Cuban Missile Crisis, before she got her vocation, all her friends were sleeping with their boyfriends since they were expecting the world to end the next day, and maybe this was a little like that. But I hope it was something slightly more positive (like love) compelling us to take off our clothes and expose all our virtues and our flaws to each other and the room in general. I sometimes think that walls know things and absorb things and remember things, and both Pavel and I think that scenes like that are written down in the Book of Life. I believe Adonai would be pleased, since Pavel and I have known each other for two and a half years, and love was involved (though we won't reveal exactly how much love or who was feeling it). The point is, I definitely have doubts about Pavel, now that we're back, and it's true that our whole relationship has always been conducted beneath a cloud of doubt, suspicion, and occasional euphoria. But at the Ho-Hum Motel, *the doubt was gone and we were Nebraskans — warm, friendly, and unsuspicious of each other's motives. I knew who Pavel was and he knew who I was.*

My mind did not drift while I was making love to him, except that I noticed that he seemed rather experienced for someone who talked so much about being indifferent to sex. But mostly I was thinking of him and how much I loved him and always had and always would. It turned out that I was the one who wasn't crazy about sex because it felt nice (nothing special) but what felt even nicer was this world we had swirled up that only we knew about and only we would ever know about — with the exception of my grandchildren reading this, to whom I am planning to leave my journals in the hope that we will clear away the thick muck of Old World silence that my family is ensconced in.

I guess happiness doesn't last (this didn't) because Pavel turned rather cold on the bus and revealed his secret plan to become a rabbi, and I just don't think I could kiss someone with a beard.

* *

Karel was working at the kitchen table on Saturday morning when Raine came in to fix her breakfast. "Guess what, Daddy?" she said.

"What, dear?"

"I've fallen in love with an astronaut."

"I thought you were in love with Pavel."

"It's a different kind of love," she said. "His name is Russell Schweickart."

"Russell Schweickart isn't an astronaut any more. He's probably old enough to be your grandfather."

"That may be true, but he speaks, and my heart sings. I've never in my whole life had that experience."

"Raine, please. Come down to earth."

"Can you think of anyone more on earth than I am? Daddy, I'm just so deeply in love with that dogwood tree that it actually discusses things with me. When you love something, it responds to you. It's one of the Seven Laws of Noah."

"Don't you have exams coming up?"

"Yes—and love is such a distraction. I mean, the things Russell Schweickart says about nuclear bombs!"

"I was hoping to get some work done today, but instead you and I are going to study," Karel said. "Up in your room. For two hours. And I don't expect to hear any complaints."

She felt like Galileo under house arrest as they walked together up the stairs. Looking at her room through her father's eyes, she noticed certain signs of sloth: wrinkled clothes on the floor, books thrown around to give the look of studiousness, her Jello Biafra poster billowing down off the wall, pillows strewn everywhere—hardly an environment in which to strive toward excellence.

* *

Pavel and I welcomed in the New Year sitting by the river, conjuring up positive points about the 20th century. We were quite good at it. By the time we got through with our assessment, you would not have thought the World Wars and the Holocaust even occurred. We both believe that Homo sapiens must look at the 20th century through a lens of hope, or we will lack the confidence to make moral progress. We began with Freud, on whom I consider myself a scholar since Vikey talked to me about him in a monologue that lasted for years. Who looked inside the human mind more deeply than he did? Well, Socrates tried to—but the point is, Hitler didn't. Stalin didn't. Pinochet didn't. We absolutely have to keep a leash on our dark side and know what it's up to, while we're also reflecting on all the progress we've made in the 20th century: penicillin was invented, lynching was condemned, schools were desegregated, blacks and women got to vote, the Nazis and the KKK were banished.

It was a fabulous start to the New Year, watching the lights twinkle on the George Washington Bridge, kissing, and planning a century built on hope. Simone Weil said that real evil is gloomy, monotonous, and barren, while imaginary evil is romantic and varied, and imaginary good is boring but real good is new, marvelous, intoxicating.

* *

As she wrapped herself in the warm folds of her quilt, Raine felt a creature like a caterpillar watching her with willowy black eyes. Behind the organdy curtains in her room, snow was falling. Crystals of ice clung to the chunk of pink quartz she kept on the windowsill. *You are a bird-cage*, a voice said to her. *Something's fluttering inside.*

She got up. The floor was freezing under her feet. When she took a bath, she tried to avoid looking in the mirror, but when she finally did look, four eyes were looking back at her. She hurried into her room and got dressed in her starched blouse and jumper, loading books and papers into her backpack, putting on her jacket and scarf and rushing down the stairs and out the front door, into the snow. The whole time, she could feel someone watching her.

She walked straight to the subway and down the steps. It was reassuring to be under the city while it snowed, in the lighted cars of the trains, with this weight above her— the city turning pale, glittering with snow, growing pure and white, flickering with diamonds.

She got off at the Bronx Botanical Garden, following the snowy paths that would lead to Pavel. The snow was stained with bee droppings. After a long walk, she saw Pavel through the whitened glass leaning over the daffodils and tulips blooming in the old snow-covered greenhouse. She wanted to go inside, but it felt better to watch him through the glass, to look at the spring flowers as the snowflakes melted on her face.

* *

Gigantic things happen to people—crazy, incredible things. But they begin as something very, very tiny that the person doesn't even notice. I think this is one of the problems in the universe.

I rarely go to school anymore. When I do, I feel like a Picasso woman with a big, square body that her roundness is growing into. Women had been round for centuries until Picasso saw something square in them. The Picasso woman is round, she is square, she is triangular, she has a conehead and one eye that sees everything.

Now I know that something was trying to get my attention for two whole months, and I was trying to ignore it. I have decided to face it with both my eyes open, look at it, and figure out what it has to say to me. But it is not at all what I had planned on. In fact, it is terrifying news that was confirmed by this clinic on Broadway that Mary and I went to. Not that it needed confirmation, because I can actually feel the speck of innocence that has taken up residence between my liver and my appendix. I realize it has been pestering me for some time. Don't think for one minute that I feel warmly toward it. I do not believe there is anything even remotely motherly about me. I am in a bad mood most of the time, and I keep taking the train up to the Bronx to tell Pavel. But then I retreat because everything inside me is assuring me that telling him is a BAD BAD idea. I want to envision him being happy, and willing to make the best of it, and us being·involved in this amazing but horrible project together. I want to envision us standing on our heads and coming up with an innovative response to our dilemma. I want to envision Mrs. Orzagh being happy, and the four of us living together in their house in the Bronx. I want to envision having a bris eight days after the baby is born, and Mary and Karel and Raisa and Janey and her mom and Mr. K. being there, and everyone eating ice cream topped with violets and feeling happy.

But I am not that imaginative. I just know Pavel will blame me, his mother's blood pressure will spiral out of control, and I will be thrown out of St. Ursula's. I can't even imagine how Mother and Daddy will react. Is it any wonder I've given up thinking?

Mary—the only one who knows, other than the lab technicians—is upset, I believe. She keeps her feelings a secret, but I can tell she doesn't mean it when she says, "A baby is always something to be celebrated—an old soul returning to the world." The only reason she seems calm is because the attitudes of Greenland came with her to New York, attitudes like Ayornamat—it cannot be helped.

I don't dare tell Mr. K. I know he'll be disappointed in me, and I also think he'll get mad at Pavel, and he may even pilfer one of the knives out of my collection and go after him. He is not the most stable guidance counselor in New York.

I hardly think he is made of the stuff a high school requires. I'm afraid he will melt into a puddle when I give him the news, like the wicked witch in The Wizard of Oz.

A wizard—that's exactly what I need! But all I have is Mary, good-hearted angel who has agreed to present the news to Dr. and Mrs. Rassaby. Yikes!

———

I rode all the way out to Coney Island and all the way up to the Cloisters, and the train was like a galloping dragon clattering and hissing along the tracks, while at home Mary was telling Raisa and Karel the news. I stayed away for an unnaturally long time, and when I returned, looking very maternal in my Wonder Woman jacket and earmuffs, I felt like Admiral Peary returning from the North Pole. Mary had fled. If I expected a bouquet of flowers, a date for the baby shower, and a congratulatory message, I must have been quite surprised to receive instead the news of a doctor's appointment for me on January 25th. Karel and Raisa did not use the word "abortion"—they referred to it as "doing something." I was speechless and ascended to my room. I guess I am naive because I never in a million years envisioned such a response to my news. It seems like such an uncreative solution from two smart people with tons of graduate degrees. What did you actually learn in college, Mother and Daddy? Apparently not reverence for life. Maybe I should not be surprised. But I am. And I didn't *even cry because I was so scared that on the morning of January 25th, the baby and I would head out of the house with Mother and Daddy, and when we came back at lunchtime, one of us would be missing. And what is absolutely macabre and chilling is that January 25th is exactly nine months before I was born — the abortion was scheduled to take place on the anniversary of my conception!*

* *

Inside the enormous buildings of the American Museum of Natural History, volunteers glued together shards of pots broken before Moses was born, beetles were used to clean hummingbird skeletons, laboratory specialists pored through data to explain the phylogeny of sea fans, the anatomy of frogs' legs, the evolution of giant ferns. Hallways were stacked to the ceiling with carefully boxed human skeletons, insects were pinned inside little boxes, sea cucumbers floated in jugs, ants were paralyzed inside Dominican amber, frogs were pickled in alcohol.

Every morning except Monday when the museum was closed, Raine joined the ten o'clock tour of the collection. She liked it that people had cared enough to re-create nature indoors, filling twenty-three Gothic buildings across from Central Park with the dried-up vestiges of life on earth.

Some days, she felt like screaming, and sometimes she thought to herself, "You *should* scream." Then she thought:

"Don't scream!" and began to wonder what the baby would look like and if there was any possibility she could be a good mother for it. One afternoon, she took Holly, the big fat baby doll she had played with as a child, strapped her into the neighbor's stroller sitting in the alleyway behind her house, and pushed her through Central Park. As she and the doll passed the children's zoo, the Delacorte Clock, and the Strawberry Fields, she repeated to herself, *your old life is gone and will never return.*

January 25th was creeping near, but she and the tour were going off in the other direction as they walked, very slowly, through the columned rooms with their ornate ceilings.

After Raine left the museum, she spent the afternoons riding the subways as they rattled and swayed and rocked through the tunnels, with Pavel somewhere above her, watering tulips, having conversations with daffodils. Sitting on the bench waiting for trains, she read the Torah. When she climbed the stairs from the subway, snow was falling, and as she walked through the park, she could feel her life forming like a snowflake around some tender unique shape that remained unseen in the universe. Mary always said that the Inuit believe there's no boundary between the possible and the impossible.

She remembered Vikey telling her about Laylah, the Angel of Night, bringing a baby before God to learn its fate, and at that moment it is written where the child will live and when it will die, whether it will be rich or poor, strong or weak, wise or foolish. Only one decision is left unwritten: whether it will be wicked or good. Then the Angel of Souls ascends to the highest heaven to bring back the soul destined for this child, and the soul enters the child and nestles under the mother's breast. A different angel teaches the soul all it will learn during its days on earth, and when it comes time for the child to be born, instantly the soul forgets everything, and the child comes into the world, crying and afraid.

The tour group walked through the Lila Acheson Wallace Wing of Mammals and Their Extinct Relatives. In a room upstairs thousands of specimens of preserved fish and toads and frogs were stored in jars on shelves with green metal partitions.

They stood gazing at the paralyzed butterflies: a wild cotton moth on swamp rose mallow, a green swallow-tail emperor moth on sweetgum, a black swallow-tail butterfly on magnolia, a royal walnut moth on persimmon. She gazed into the tiny glass butterfly eyes. Everything was still. Only she was moving.

* *

Now I must describe Peter. He is the tour guide I am getting to know quite well—a paleontologist at the museum. His eyes are a gingery turquoise. He's tall, slightly stooped, and his hair sticks up like feathers. The museum unearths magnificent mysteries, he says. It skirts the fringes of the unknown. He stands in front of groups of people, enumerating the major innovations in the evolution of mammals: watertight eggs, eye sockets, hooves, placentas, and stirrup-shaped stapes. I love the idea that dinosaurs try to keep their secrets from paleontologists. Peter is fascinated with the same things I am: the gels, evaporated seas, and coastal shallows out of which life creeps. I talk to him after the tours. He listens very carefully, as though he speaks another language and is trying to figure out what I'm saying. I could not resist telling him I was pregnant and the surprising thing is that when I said it, both of us were shocked. The news was so stark, modern, and flabbergasting in comparison to the dusty, dignified lives of the dead dinosaurs. When I told Peter, he could not even look me in the eye, but I could tell by his reaction that he thinks it's REALLY bad news. We were standing in the Hall of Saurischian Dinosaurs. What he said without saying it is that this isn't something you're going to make all right, Raine Marie Rassaby, with your absolutely preposterous romantic fly-by-night notions. His eyes say everything he can't put into words, probably because of all that time he spent in the Gobi Desert. He is so deep I can well imagine myself falling in, but I think it is just his kindness I'm attracted to because this is a human attribute that is in great scarcity at the moment, and when I feel even a modicum of it, I go lolloping into that person's life. I have thought of calling up Ms. Violet Wells in Sunflower City, Nebraska, merely because I feel she'd be sympathetic, and I need to get my doses of kindness from people who are not of the male persuasion, at least until the baby arrives. (If he or she is going to arrive, which now seems doubtful.) I simply cannot fall in love with Peter. Can you picture him going to the card store and picking me out a funny card and mailing it, just because it would make me happy? No! Can you picture him dropping by to see me not because he wants something but because I might be lonely and scared? No! Can you picture him being by my side when the stork arrives with my unwanted baby? No! He's too busy labeling bones and gazing at the contours of creatures who have been dead for sixty-five million years. His smile reminds me of the oviraptor embryo at the museum, squished into an eggshell, with its rounded yellow beak and its chin leaning on a floppy paw. Peter does not look as though he knows anything about pregnancy, or babies, or even sex, so I must depend upon my own counsel.

"I'll be pregnant only very temporarily, if my parents get their way," I said to him yesterday. "They're quite despotic. They could talk a hungry dog out of a pork chop. Some nights, I go down to dinner wearing earplugs."

He smiled, and I said, "If I do have an abortion, I'm planning a ceremony in my garden for the baby. Maybe I'll invite you. It will be a very, very, very, very sad occasion.

I'm planning to purchase five dozen half-dead tulips, and at the end we'll throw them up in the air, and they'll flutter down over us like we're at the opera. It will be a terrible event—not exactly the burying of a baby but the burying of a baby's hopes."

* *

Mary had arranged lilies and roses in a crystal bowl. The wine glasses were gleaming in candlelight. Behind Karel's chair were paintings of an ivory-billed woodpecker and a red-eyed vireo. The windows were framed with scallops of snow.

"I read that Audubon killed those birds, then he painted them and made them look like they were alive," Raine said. Her parents said nothing. She pretended she was a paleontologist observing the two of them sitting in their formal king-and-queen postures, like Macbeth and Lady Macbeth: shoulders thrown back, diamond earrings, ruby tie-pin, a brown frosting of lipstick, mysterious candlelit eyes.

The Torah was open on her lap, and she read aloud, "And it came to pass after these things, that God tested Abraham and said, 'Abraham.' And he said, 'Here I am.' And He said, 'Take your son, your only son, the one you love, Isaac, and go into the land of Moriah and offer him there for a burnt offering upon one of the mountains which—'"

"You've remembered what tomorrow is?" her mother said. "Haven't you?"

Raine shrugged, and Mary came into the room with platters of pot roast, potatoes, and green beans. Mary refused to look at Raine or offer her any moral support, and very faintly, Raine could hear her grandmother singing, *Double, double, toil and trouble, fire burn and cauldron bubble*. Hunched into a ball, the baby was listening.

"Daddy, I love it that you fell in love with stars when you were my age," Raine said. "And you've spent your whole life studying them, and that's what I feel like we all have to do—love something so much that we feel accountable for its demise."

He smiled at her. She was making a design of a Jewish star with her green beans. "I read about a man who dropped the bomb on Hiroshima," she said. "And you know what he said? These are his exact words. 'I had seen a city down there. People were moving. Then when I looked back after we had leveled out, all I could see was boiling black tar with steam above it.'"

"That's a terrible thing," Karel said. "But I guess he had no choice."

"What do you mean?"

"He was a military pilot, and we were at war."

"But Daddy, did you hear what he said? He dropped

this bomb, and a city full of people turned to boiling black tar. Don't you think he has any responsibility for that?"

"No—I don't."

"Then it's okay to do whatever the government tells you to do?"

"In a case like that, of course," he said.

"Even if it's against your deepest morals?" Raine said.

"Yes."

"So people should have obeyed Hitler? They should have obeyed Stalin? What about the Nuremberg trials? Didn't the judges reject the idea that only a state and not individuals could be guilty of war crimes?"

"Raine, you have more important things to think about right now," Raisa said.

"Well, I can't see how my baby's going to have a future if people go around saying people have permission to drop nuclear bombs on other people!"

"Raine," Raisa said, tipping her head to the side as though she were about to pick up her violin. "It isn't a baby—it's a *fetus*. And you're not a woman—you're a girl. A very immature one."

"Well, the baby's immature, too, so the two of us will have a little something in common," Raine said, standing up and putting her hands on her hips.

"A baby needs two parents, a home, an income, and the possibility of a decent future," Raisa said.

"A decent future?" Raine said. "You think floating around in formaldehyde is preferable to living a life with me!" She threw her napkin down, ran up the stairs, and posted her *No Trespassing* sign on the door. She went into the bathroom where pots of geraniums sat on a shelf above the tub, ran a steaming hot bath, and undressed, slipping into the water and thinking of lighting the Sabbath candles because in Jewish custom it has always been women who begin the Sabbath, who provide the light. She poured a cupful of water over her head, and it was like dropping from childhood into adulthood because when she floated down into the water, she was a teenager and when she stood up and picked up a thick pink towel, she had become a mother.

She realized that she had never gone very far out of her way for anyone—not for her grandmother, or her parents, or even for Pavel. She was the center of her world, but in the bathtub, everything changed because her child was threatened and therefore there was a tiny change in the way she saw herself, and she believed that when something tiny changes in your life, everything begins to change.

She picked up the towel, and suddenly she could feel a tiny boy floating inside her like a white gardenia. She reached over and took some dirt out of the geranium pot, and she closed her eyes and vowed that, no matter what, she would never give her baby up, and she spoke up for him with her whole being, with every muscle and every cell and every thought and belief that she had, and then she sank back down into the soapy water and swallowed the dirt and prayed.

IV

Raine was in bed, studying the ice on the tree branches outside her window, remembering the year she had painted her room black. When she came home from school one day, someone, without telling her, had repainted the room white. She would allow her baby to paint his room any color he wanted.

The sun rose, and she heard Mary in the kitchen, then fell asleep and awakened to her parents' steps in the hall. She got up, put on her skeleton costume, and walked down the stairs. Raisa looked up as Raine bounded into the room. "You're a little late for Halloween," she said.

"I believe my skeleton costume has a role to play in this astonishing morning," Raine said. "Good morning, Mary! Mother and Daddy, sit down—I have an announcement to make."

"We are sitting down," Karel said.

"Sorry—I memorized this speech, and in the speech, you were standing up."

Plates of scrambled eggs, toast, and fried ham were spread out on the table. But no one was eating.

"It's just a fact I'd like to present to you," Raine said. "Remember Vikey's favorite proverb? 'Do and undo—the day is long enough.'"

"All right," Karel said. "Let's hear it."

"But I don't want you to get mad," Raine said.

"Out with it, Raine," Karel said.

Raine closed her eyes and said, "I'm sure you both mean well, but I could not possibly kill my baby."

"You can't kill something that doesn't exist," Raisa said.

"But he does exist. He's a boy, and his name is Lamont."

"Lamont?" Karel said.

"Lamont Rassaby—your grandchild. I've decided to welcome him into the world. Like you did with me."

Raisa began speaking with the accent she used when she was very, very upset—a hint of Scottish picked up at her Glasgow concerts combined with the old rhythms of Slovakia. Raine suddenly thought of how excited Vikey would be about the baby. She imagined Vikey buying presents for him and maternity clothes for her, and having a party, and telling her that it wasn't essential to graduate from high school. What was important was to live a noble life.

Raine could not listen to her mother anymore, so she left the house, ran through the snowy garden, down the alleyway, and up West 88th Street all the way to the park. The trees were glazed with ice. She wasn't wearing a coat, but she wasn't cold, and she didn't care what people thought of her costume. The baby was somersaulting to the rhythm of her anger, turning something horrible into something wonderful—because that's what babies do.

It was hard for her to feel so bewildered when she was about to become a mother. Would she pass on to her baby all the silence and confusion she had inherited? Would she fill him with her fears instead of her loves?

* *

Pavel was hanging by his legs from the lowest branch of the leafless dogwood tree, the ice was melting, the sun was growing warmer, and on the windowsill in the kitchen, azalea plants were blooming. "Did your mother tell you I called you about six hundred times?" Raine said, looking up at him, upside down, in the tree.

"No. She didn't."

"Where have you been, Pavel?"

"Working. Getting ready to go to Israel."

"How come you haven't come around?"

"Because I'm leaving next month, and I don't think we should make saying goodbye into a sad event."

"Do you still feel the same way about making love to me?" she said.

"What do you mean?"

"I mean, it was wonderful, wasn't it?"

"The first time, no. The second time, it was good. The third time—"

"Pavel, if you had to choose between me and your mother, who would you choose?"

"My mother is pretty amazing. My dad didn't leave any

insurance or savings because he wasn't planning to die and she just had this secretarial job. She saves a lot of money for me. She never buys herself anything."

"So you'd choose her?"

"Probably."

"Then we might be in trouble."

He dropped down out of the tree and looked at her. "What kind of trouble?"

"You know that trip we took in November? It was a lot more complicated than it seemed."

"What do you mean?" he said.

"We're having a baby."

He sat down on the wrought-iron bench. He crossed his legs, then uncrossed them, then crossed them again. He looked at her, he looked at his fingernails, he looked at her again. Then he started biting his nails.

"It took me a long time to realize it," she said. "I'm three months pregnant. I never knew you could get pregnant with condoms. As soon as I met you, I just wanted to be a squishy little girl with you, but you always wanted me to be a tomboy."

Pavel wasn't looking at her. He was staring at the tree.

"Remember how you didn't even call me or send me a Valentine?" she said. "The baby sent me a message that was like the Valentine I didn't get from you."

"You're telling me this news after it's too late to do anything about it?"

"*Pavel.* Our baby is listening to this conversation."

"It's not a baby. It's only the possibility of a baby. It's like a map—not a place." He put his head in his hands. Then he looked up at her and said, "So you're *sure*?"

"I'm positive."

"What will I tell my mother?"

"I don't know," she said. "The truth, I guess."

They were silent for a moment, then she said, "How come you waited to tell me you were planning to become a rabbi? I mean, you invited me to Nebraska, then we had sex, then you told me about wanting to be a rabbi."

"I thought we should sleep on the bus. Going to that motel was your idea."

"But you wanted to, right?"

"I just wish you had warned me," he said.

"Warned you about what?"

"That you were fertile."

"Why didn't you warn me that *you* were fertile?" she said.

He stood up and started walking in circles around the tree. "Raine, I just don't know what to say. I feel like somebody came and put a bag over my head."

"How do you think I feel, Pavel?"

"How *do* you feel?"

"I don't know," she said. "Physically, I feel okay, but mentally I feel like I'm being carried into the woods by some horrible monster."

"How would you like to open your eyes on your first day on earth and discover we were your parents?"

"I don't think that's so bad," she said.

"So you've known about this for a while. And what was the reason you didn't tell me?"

"I was afraid to," she said. "I started skipping school, and I used to take the subway up to the greenhouses. I saw you inside, but I couldn't go in."

"Why couldn't you?"

"Because I didn't know how you'd react, and I didn't trust you to be happy about the baby, like I was."

"I thought you said it was like being dragged into the woods by a horrible monster."

"I'm trying to be happy about it. It is a miraculous thing."

He sat down and said, "Well, I can't marry you, but I can probably do something. I just got my paycheck. Maybe I could buy it some clothes."

"Make them blue," she said. "It's a boy."

"How do you know?"

"I just do. His name is Lamont."

"*Lamont?*"

"Yes. Lamont. We could hyphenate our names. Lamont Rassaby-Orzagh or Lamont Orzagh-Rassaby."

"This is like a nightmare," he said.

"Will you please not call Lamont a nightmare?"

"I'm just being honest," he said. "You've always been so full of yourself. You think you know everything. Look at you—suddenly you're acting so mature."

She ordered herself not to cry and said, "Are you really going shopping for Lamont?"

"I guess I'll have to. You're making me feel like a creep."

"Come back later and we'll look at the stuff together. It will be kind of fun."

"Or kind of depressing," he said, and he laughed, but it wasn't really laughter. It was more like the shofar blowing Shevarim: three broken notes that sounded like sobbing.

* *

I finally went to dinner at the distinguished rabbi Pavel Orzagh's house. He hadn't told his mother about the baby, so it was awkward, and I just felt like shouting out, "We're having a baby, and Pavel's not going to Israel!" I could picture being taken into Mrs. Orzagh's blubbery arms and being danced around the house. But instead Pavel's eyes were hopping all over the room, he was biting his nails, his mother was watching me quite warily. I felt really guilty, like I was about to ruin their nice calm life. I felt like it was my fault for adulterating rabbi material. Pavel and I have plans to create a better world, and I have confidence in them, but I could just feel his mother's counter-plans for him hovering over me like the pope lowering a boulder onto Saint Euphemia.

The Orzaghs' dining room reminded me of Freud's study with its violet air and its lace doilies and its simmering candles burning in memory of something. I looked at the photographs in the hutch of Pavel on a tricycle, Pavel on a swing, Pavel playing in a band, Pavel dancing with his mother at one of the picnics. I loved looking at the menorah and the tsedakah box on the bookshelf. I looked down at Pavel's mother's thick, silky legs and pictured Pavel sliding out from between them and looking up at her with his burning green eyes. I loved the house with its aura of Seders and Purims, of cleansings and celebrations, and I admired Mrs. Orzagh, with her pink nylon dress and her excessive-ness in the kitchen and her way of laughing at practically everything Pavel said.

It was like being in Israel and carrying on something that is very, very ancient. There Pavel and Mrs. Orzagh were, looking at me like I was the seductress of the rabbi — and let us not forget what it says in the Talmud about the necessity of stonings. The thought of how much I loved Pavel was devoid from the room, and it was all about finger-pointing, a territory I am more than familiar with. I felt like a punk again, hanging around in the streets with everyone looking at me and talking about me and women coming up and lecturing me about my outfit and men coming up and propositioning me. Pavel was NOT looking at me, and Mrs. Orzagh WAS — with tidy little dachshund eyes. I wanted to protest, I wanted to defend myself, but I was speechless because their accusations were silent ones and how can you defend yourself against silence? I wanted to explain why I was attending a Catholic high school, and how in spite of my years of servitude in CCD, I have actually read the Torah, all five books, at least fifteen times, and how my grandmother never celebrated Hanukkah because it was a minor holiday — but she did practice Tashlich on the first day of Rosh Hashanah, going down to the Hudson and emptying her pockets of lint and breadcrumbs and casting her sins into the river.

The candlelit room grew dimmer and dimmer and dimmer, and I desperately wanted a look of approval from Pavel, but he withheld that and all other signs of warmth. Dr. Hadcock says it's draining to be with people we have to impress, but I have to admit I was completely taken in by the scene because the dining room with Pavel and his mother and the mahogany table and silver candlesticks and menorah was exactly what I wanted for myself and my child. I wished we could go there every week and sit at the table and eat matzo ball soup and chestnut cake while Mrs. Orzagh jiggled the baby on her lap and laughed at his antics. I tried to picture a room upstairs wallpapered with happy lion faces. I wanted everyone to be excited and to act like Lamont was someone to be celebrated. Weren't the shofar blasts meant to arouse our slothful selves to new possibilities?

Now that I'm back in my bedroom, I can think of everything I should have said to the Ice Cube Queen and the Ice Cube Prince, but at the time, I only wanted to please them. Why does it always seem like the people who are the meanest and most critical are always the ones we try the hardest to please? Pavel never does one thing to please me. Why didn't he walk me to the subway? Because he had to help his mother with the dishes. So I went walking alone down Pugsley Avenue at night carrying an innocent baby under my puffy party dress. Raine, you talk a lot about Americans being asleep, but when do you plan to wake up? For over two years, this guy has fed you exactly the amount you need to keep from starving, and not one bite more. He does not want to expend effort—he just wants to help himself to Mary's chocolate-chip cookies, to say nothing of your bazumas and fertile eggs.

Here is our paltry dinner conversation:

"Pavel tells me you're planning to deface a nuclear weapon," Mrs. O. said.

"It's not exactly defacing because a nuclear weapon doesn't have a face," I replied. "But if it did, it would be a lot easier. I mean, if you met a bear on the path and looked into its eyes, you'd at least have a chance to connect or communicate or plead for your life. You and the bear might have something in common. But if you met a nuclear weapon on the path, all you'd be meeting is a mindless ball *of plutonium."*

Mrs. Orzagh waved her arms in the air. "Political schmetical!" she exclaimed. "We can't go out and save the world."

"Pavel and I don't want to save the world," I said. "We want to save ourselves."

Mrs. Orzagh was munching on her honey cake in tiny bites, looking at her cake, then looking at me, then looking back at her cake.

"The problem with young people is that they don't spend time reading the Torah like my Pavel does," she said. I was trying really hard to commiserate with all three of us. I pictured Pavel with long sideburns, wearing a tallith. I pictured myself as Yokheved, saving Moses' life by putting him in a reed basket and sailing him down the river. I pictured Mrs. Orzagh as an animal—and what animal would want her offspring venturing out onto the savannah and doing dangerous things?

We seemed to be just having dinner, but really, everything was at stake. It wasn't enough for me to put on Vikey's flax apron and light the Sabbath candles. I needed to follow the tradition of earning my womanhood by sacrificing something for my child. I could feel myself quickly sinking in Mrs. Orzagh's estimation, and all the time I was sinking, I was loving more and more being in her dining room, inhaling the scent of burning candles and red cabbage boiled in vinegar.

* *

Raine and Al stood by the window in Al's office, watching the wind blowing up whitecaps in the river. "You mean Frieda is divorcing you because of one crummy arrest?" Raine said.

"My getting arrested was a culmination of a long period in which Frieda and I were running on separate tracks, Raine. Let's talk about something else."

"You're not going to jail, are you?"

"I haven't gone to court yet. And what about you? Where have you been? You've missed a lot of school."

"I have some news, Mr. K."

"Okay."

"It's not good news."

"It usually isn't," he said.

"You've been really nice, cheering me on toward graduation and everything, so I wanted you to be the first to know. The first at St. Ursula's, anyway. Sometimes I think of it as exciting news. But it's hard to feel one way about it because it's so complicated. Sometimes I'm happy about it, sometimes I'm sad, sometimes I'm mad, and sometimes I'm completely freaking out—"

"Get to the point, Raine."

"When I went to Nebraska with Pavel in November, we came back with a souvenir. A baby. I'm pregnant." Chills ran through her every time she said the word. She wondered if there was some other way to present the news. *I'm with child. I'm in the family way. I'm in an interesting condition.* "I'm not really panicky about it, though," she continued. "I have it sort of arranged in my head. My relationship with Pavel started out as a fantasy, then we went on that bus trip and our relationship became real. Then it got false again. Now I don't even know if Pavel is a real fake or a fake fake."

The undersides of the waves were an icy green. He had always wanted to join the Polar Bear Club, standing on the shore in the winter, then diving into the freezing river with a group of happy people. "I don't know what to say, Raine. This is the last thing I expected."

"I'm really okay with the whole thing. Last year in school, I took a course in parenthood, and we had to carry a bag of potatoes with us everywhere we went. So I feel I'm somewhat prepared."

"A bag of potatoes doesn't need its diapers changed," he said irritably. "Its teeth aren't crooked, and it doesn't have to be rushed to the hospital in the middle of a blizzard."

She moved away from him. "I can't believe how obtuse you're being—just like everyone else!"

Al felt dazed. He had no idea how to respond. "Okay," he said. "I'm sorry. Please sit down. Can I help in some way?"

"When I first found out I was pregnant, I hung around

the museum a lot, where these caterpillars in glass jars were eating huge chunks out of leaves, and I was trying to make myself realize that someday soon, this hungry fetus would be doing the same thing to me. I was afraid to tell Pavel, and I was spending a lot of time in the celery bin, but when I went to the museum, I tried to look at my pathetic situation through the ribs of an 11,000-year-old mastodon. When I picture the world full of flying reptiles, my problems seem a lot more trivial. Unexpected horrible things happen, but unexpected happy things happen, too. I met this very interesting paleontologist, Peter, and decided I'd like to turn Pavel in and have Peter instead as the baby's father. But he wasn't really interested in the baby or me. He's rather involved with dinosaurs."

"So when is this, is this—"

"In August. It will either be a Virgo or a Leo. A Virgo is perfectionistic and fault-finding, quiet, intellectual, nervous, and sensitive. What sign are you, Al?"

"Capricorn," he said. He was chewing on the end of his pen.

"Capricorns are young when they're old and old when they're young," she said. "If the baby's a Leo, he'll be a show-off. Blunt, outspoken, romantic, egotistical, tempera-mental, and domineering. Leos like to be in the spotlight."

"But what will you do, Raine?"

She laughed and said, "I don't know, Mr. K. What will

you do?"

"I have no idea," he said.

"You know what? The flatware in our drawer is slowly disappearing. We're down to two forks and a spoon."

* *

"Goodbye, Raine," Pavel said. "Mazel Tov."

The white rock cress was blooming along the garden wall beside a patch of daffodils. Raine was sitting on the iron bench. Pavel was standing by the garden gate. "I'd like us to continue to be friends, and I hope you'll let me know what happens with the baby."

"What do you mean by that?"

"I have to leave, but I don't want there to be any hard feelings. I'm not saying goodbye just because I'm going to Israel." He opened the gate and walked into the garden. "I think there has to be trust between two people."

"So, are you saying you don't trust me?" she said.

"I imagine, knowing you, that you wanted to get pregnant. You're hell-bent to have this baby, the same way you're always hell-bent to have your way about everything."

"You're just mad because we're not doing this your way."

"You knew I was planning to go to rabbinical school."

"I did *not* know. And maybe people who are planning to become rabbis shouldn't have sex!" She started to cry. "Pavel, what's wrong with you? You seem so spiteful all of a sudden."

"I want to do the right thing, Raine, and I've been thinking a lot about what the right thing is. It's all I think about. And I resent that, too. I'm getting the feeling that this is *your* agenda for *my* life."

"Sometimes I get mad at the baby, too. I think it's mean, but I can't help it."

"When I first saw you at the picnics, I wish I had gone running in the other direction."

Raine began walking in circles around the glass table, feeling as though she were hearing things. She wanted to run upstairs and get her earplugs, but instead she calmed herself down with images floating through her mind of Mary and Russell Schweickart. "Pavel, I don't think we should turn on each other like this," she said. "It's too sad. I never thought we'd be having a conversation as awful as this. If you decided you wanted to leave me and the baby and go to Israel, I could kind of understand it because you and your mom have been planning that and talking about it for a long time. Even if you decided you don't want to hang around with me forever, I could understand it. I really could."

"When I'm in an unsettled place in myself, I stop dreaming. I haven't had a dream since you told me about the baby. And I need to pay attention to that. I hope you understand. I haven't had a dream in three weeks. Besides, I don't really believe in teenagers getting married."

"I don't want to marry you, Pavel. I'm planning to marry

someone else."

"Who?"

"He's an astronaut I met in Alabama."

"When were you in Alabama?" he asked.

"When I was at camp."

"When you were a kid?"

"I spent every summer in Alabama between 1990 and 1993, and he came to talk to us. I remember him quite well."

"Oh, that's a good one," he said. "Why'd you pick an astronaut? So he can join you in outer space?"

"I picked him because he is a man with moral vision. Unlike some people I know."

"What's his name?" he said.

"Russell Schweickart."

"Russell Schweickart? The guy who went to the moon?"

"Russell Schweickart did not go to the moon. He was an astronaut in the first lunar module."

"In the sixties?" he said.

"In 1969."

"How old is he?"

"What do you care, Pavel?"

"He was an astronaut in 1969? That was thirty years ago."

"Age is irrelevant to me. I don't even care if you go to Israel, because your being the baby's father is just a technicality. I thought you were this compassionate, visionary man, but you're not what I thought you were."

"And you're not what I thought you were. You're unbelievably flaky, Raine. Leave it to you to be in love with someone who's fifty years older than you."

"Grow lungs and legs and relocate, Pavel!" She pulled the French doors open and glared at him. "You'll make a great rabbi—one of those big fat egos in a yarmulke covered with jewels, all wrapped up in your fringed garment!"

She went into the kitchen, slammed the door behind her as hard as she could, and ran upstairs, put her *No Trespassing* sign on the door, and wrote in black ink on a sheet of white paper:

Mrs. Raisa Rassaby and Dr. Karel Rassaby
announce that the engagement of their daughter,
Raine Marie, to Mr. Pavel Orzagh
has been terminated by mutual consent.

* *

Al heard a *ping* on his window. He put his book down on the coffee table in his den. He didn't move. He wondered if it was a bullet and imagined someone getting shot in the empty lot below his window. Would he run outside to help? Would he pursue the criminal? Or would he stay in his den, sneaking a look through the shades and waiting for someone else to respond? He listened for screams or grunts or sirens. Nothing. Another *ping*. He walked to the window and saw Raine standing three floors below, waving up at him. He slid open the window and storm window and stuck his head out.

"For God's sake, Raine," he said. "Are you trying to break my window?"

"Can I come up, Al? Boy trouble!"

"No. Frieda would have a fit."

"Frieda's back?" she said.

"No, she isn't back. But I'm a man living alone now, and it would be very unprofessional for me to invite a student up to my apartment."

"You didn't invite me. I invited myself. *Please,* Al."

"I'll come down."

He went down the stairs, wishing she wasn't such a nuisance—yet he felt sorry for her when she fell sobbing into his arms. "I've messed everything up!" she said.

"No, you haven't."

"I *have*—big-time. I wish I was dead."

"Maybe you do right now—but it will pass," he said.

"I put all this energy into Pavel and now he's gone, and I wanted to make my parents happy, but you never saw two people look more miserable. They're not even speaking to me."

"I'm sure your parents are quite upset about the baby, Raine. They need some time to get used to the idea. You can't blame them."

"You know what, Al? I spend all this time blaming my parents when I know who's really to blame. I am. I had doubts about Pavel, and I ignored them. I can't become a mother. I'm too selfish. I never think of anyone but myself. I can't identify with the baby. I've *really* tried. I'm terrified of childbirth. I just want somebody to clunk me over the head and wake me up when it's over. And the worst thing is I'm afraid I'll feel very lukewarm toward the baby. I just know I won't love him."

"Raine, where is that harsh voice coming from? Look at you. Please don't cry. You're shivering. Come upstairs. I'll make you some hot chocolate."

They climbed the three flights of stairs to his apartment, walked through the white living room, and sat in the kitchen overlooking the garden. The song "There Is a Rose in Spanish Harlem" had been trailing through Al's head for days.

"Raine," he said, as he stirred the cocoa on the stove, "I used to drink Scotch every night, and I'd get myself into this mood where I couldn't feel much of anything. Then one night last fall, I put my glass down, and I didn't pick it up again. I needed to get out of the house, so every evening, I walked up to the Harlem Home for the Elderly, where Frieda works. I stood outside, across the street, and looked in the windows. Then I started following Daniel Wadhams home. Remember? I didn't feel great about it, but I started to get glimpses of who I was and what I had become. And you know what, Raine? I had turned into my mother." He poured the cocoa into a white cup and placed it down before her. "Now, why would you imitate a woman who couldn't make room for anyone else in her life—who didn't take care of her son, could never get herself to do the hard thing, and drank herself to death? When I was drinking, I was dreaming. I wasn't growing. I wasn't changing. I wasn't responding."

"Oh my God," she said. "Do you feel like you've ruined your whole life?"

He laughed. "I don't know. Maybe I have." They gazed into their cocoa for a while. "Frieda never seemed to notice how much I was drinking," he said. "Of course, she's been working the night shift for years. Maybe she noticed, but she never said anything."

"Hitler blamed everybody else for his problems, too. But don't feel bad. I used to have a lot of hope for myself. Then I went to Nebraska with Pavel, and my bug collided with my windshield."

"Yes, but you're still very young."

"I used to have a lot more hope for humanity. I was a big believer in human moral evolution, but I've found out that if you don't believe in yourself, you can't believe in humanity either. And if you don't believe, you'll never accomplish one single thing. You'll be a bogo and a nogo." She refilled her cup. "Pavel deserted me yesterday. He's going to Israel to become a rabbi. He climbed the mountain of spotlessness and left me at the bottom."

"What about the baby?" he said.

"Pavel doesn't feel responsible for him, and the really, *really* scary part is I don't know if I do either."

"What do you mean?"

"I don't think I have it in me, Al. I've always been afraid that I won't live my beliefs. But the hypocrisy is much more chilling than I thought it would be."

"What do you mean, Raine? Don't cry. *Please.*" He reached in his pocket and handed her his handkerchief.

"I mean, Pavel isn't who I thought he was. But I'm not who I thought I was either. I'm too scared to have a baby. I'm afraid of the pain. I'm a truly ersatz person because I don't really believe in abortion, but if it wasn't too late, maybe I *would* have one. Vikey always said it's very easy to believe in something and very hard to practice what we believe. She was right about so many things. I wish I had been better to her."

"Raine, please. Don't cry. Here, have a cookie."

"I had this bad premonition. One night I woke up in my room, and this enormous monster was sitting in the tree outside my window, and I closed the window, but it wouldn't go away. It just kept sitting there, with this slick green face, and I finally opened the window and told him to bugger off, and he communicated to me the news that I wasn't going to love my baby. That I'd just be pretending."

"When fear talks, cowards listen," he said. "That's what my grandmother always said."

"I *am* a coward."

"No, you're not."

"I have a head full of meteors and dinosaur eggs," she said.

"You have a head full of wonderful visions. I can just hear you singing lullabies to your baby."

"You mean like, '*Oh, we'll all go together when it comes*'?" she said.

"You're going to be a dynamite mom, Raine. You have all the freshness of youth. The hell with Pavel. You and the baby can grow up together." He passed her the plate of cookies and said, "I feel absolutely awful when you cry."

"I'm sorry. I'm dumping all this stuff on you, and here you are, trying to cope with your own graumy life."

"It's okay. There's nothing as bad for me as sitting around thinking about my wife and her multiple lovers."

"I'm really scared, Al. And on top of that, I hate Pavel. I absolutely *hate* him. He was such a counterfeit person and such a phony. One time we were up in my room, and he plopped this black witch's wig on my head—he just grabbed it out of my closet and put it on my head and he had his camera with him and he took my picture with the wig on. And I knew it was because he wanted to talk himself into thinking I was ugly, and it was a very, very, *very* ugly moment between us. But I didn't say anything to him about it. You might have had your head in a Scotch bottle, but I've had my head in the Pavel trough since I was sixteen, and I spent all my time going *glug, glug, glug.*"

"Your life isn't ruined. It just has to be respected. The word respect means to look again. Nothing is as bleak as it seems. Please don't worry."

"You know what, Al? I feel really lost. Pavel used to be the parachute that lowered me into the green field."

He stood in the doorway, reluctant to close the door behind her. He listened to the gentle tapping of her footsteps on the stairs as they gradually melded into the sounds of the city.

* *

On the morning of his trial, Al walked into St. Malachy's Church near Morningside Park and sat in a pew. Women were hunched in the front rows, praying. An old man was following the Stations of the Cross. Al looked up at Jesus on the crucifix over the altar. He pictured wet butterflies, fresh out of chrysalises, hanging from sticky milkweed plants. He realized his grandmother's religion was based on the process of things turning into other things. Years earlier, he had believed in her God, but who was God to him now? As a child, he had prayed for so much, especially that he and his mother would move out of the boarding house and rent a bungalow on the beach at Breezy Point. He recited novenas and rosaries. She would stop drinking. They would be happy. He loved the words *Knock and the door will be opened.*

But the door had not opened—not for him, not for his mother, not for any of the residents of Mrs. Cobelle's boarding house. And yet, after his grandmother died, he had had a sense of being taken care of by a power that might possibly be called God. At first, he felt completely alone. He had no friends—only a few acquaintances from his six years at N.Y.U. He asked the Dooley brothers to take care of the animals and moved to a hostel in Greenwich Village, unable to bear the thought of sleeping alone in the farmhouse. He walked the streets of Manhattan with a crumpled party invitation in his back pocket. The host was a young woman he had occasionally talked to in statistics class. He didn't intend to go to her party, but at the last minute, he changed his mind and walked down to Prince Street and stood outside the apartment building. Finally, he climbed the old stairs toward the music and voices and laughter. The stairwell smelled of the rosewater his grandmother had worn. He opened the door and there Frieda was, standing by the piano in a red dress.

She was in her last year of nursing school, and soon after his grandmother's funeral, he began waiting for her outside class with a bouquet of flowers, accompanying her to the cafeteria, and walking her home at the end of the day. On several occasions, he stood singing beneath her window, and she laughed and came running down the stairs to tell him to stop. She had never met anyone like him, she said.

His dreams of a happy life with his mother had been vague, but meeting Frieda—her cherry-red dress, her smile, their long walks from Greenwich Village to Chelsea, where she lived, holding hands and talking, the day of their engagement at the Mayflower Hotel—all of it was so much more vivid than anything he could have imagined. If such an experience was not furnished by God—and wasn't God a human word?—then it at least suggested to him some comforting design in the universe.

Now, the church soothed him: the lilies in a vase on the altar, the lit candles. He did not want his ancestors— those hard-working Roman Catholic farm people—to think of him as the heathen he probably was. Yet hadn't a thread of faith remained alive in him, and isn't that why the Mother Superior had hired him? He did not need to know who God was. He was confused by all the incongruities in the Bible, and he wasn't sure that any book could describe God because books were composed of words and he did not believe language could explain the deep and inscrutable mysteries of the universe. But kneeling in the pew before the crucifix of the suffering Jesus, it was a relief for him to know that he believed in something.

* *

Birds never developed large brains because they were able to solve their problems by flying away. But other creatures, too weak or too small to flee from danger, had to face life in one place, and in Al's case, the place was a courtroom. Carved into the oak paneling were the words of Oliver Wendell Holmes: *The law is the witness and external deposit of our moral life. Its history is the history of the moral development of the race.*

The slow pace of the proceedings reminded him of the Sundays in childhood when the priest came to visit his grandmother, and he sat with them in the sunny living room. The priest did most of the talking. Al never said anything, nor did he remember either of them ever asking him a question. He loved the feeling of his grandmother beside him, the rough wool of the sweaters she wore, summer and winter. Sunlight shone through the window onto the priest's bald head, his grandmother's white hair, and the tray of flowered teacups. Sometimes the rain pounded on the tin roof above them as they drank tea, and he felt happy when his grandmother went into the kitchen to get another plate of cakes, for this meant that the priest would stay longer.

Al had on the dark suit he wore to weddings and funerals. Frieda was sitting in the visitors' section, and Al could not help thinking of the way the clock had turned, taking him from that night fourteen years ago when the lamplight shone on her hair as she stood by the piano and he had known immediately that he loved her, until she was seated here, again in a red dress, a spectator at his trial. Someday they would meet in divorce court and attempt to answer their questions, but could words ever accurately describe the demise of love? Was it his drinking, his self-ishness, his insularity? Was it Frieda's affair or the deceit surrounding it? Was it the accumulation of silence? What had happened to them? Why had they parted?

Al felt as though he were on trial for all his transgres-sions, and that in a short time, the judge would know about his selfishness as a husband, his theft of Raine's journal, his following Daniel through the streets, his need to be a savior to his high school students, imagining them writing him letters of gratitude on perfumed stationery years after their graduation. Yet, sitting there in his carved wooden chair, he felt strangely innocent.

He wished some great principle or ideal had propelled him into the courtroom—but he was just a thief, one of many whose case would come up before the judge in the course of the day. He wondered if laws necessarily created a more moral climate. Could a law encourage goodness, or did goodness have to arise in the heart? Were human beings perfectible? Was it a human obligation to face the intricacies of moral responsibility? Was there a difference between goodness and responsibility?

His lawyer spoke, saying something about Al being a decent, well-intentioned man. Al wanted to talk about his marriage, about how Frieda looked standing by the piano that night on Prince Street, how he had somehow known her then but did not know her now. The courtroom was silent. Having courage meant turning the mind to relentlessly seek or face the truth. The gavel fell. The judge spoke. Al was sure he was looking at Frieda. He hardened, then softened. Al was a free man.

* *

Oh my God, St. Ursula's Girls Against the Atomic Bomb is being taken over by horse thieves! Janey's nice to everyone, and all of us love her, but she doesn't seem to be able to get these activists to act. When St. Ursula's Girls Against the Atomic Bomb was just a dream of mine, it was almost better (not for the nuclear stockpile, maybe, but for me) because now I feel like other people have absconded with the group, and even though this is what I always wanted, it makes me feel kind of bereft. I myself never feel confident enough to drag myself up to the podium and say everything I feel in my heart. I just sit there at the meetings, quite paralyzed and beady-eyed like a cockroach eyeing a toast crumb through a crack in the wall but not having the nerve to march into somebody's kitchen. When are we going to start talking about ways to eliminate nuclear bombs?

Everybody sits there, fooling with their hair and discussing their love lives. They all seem suspicious of Sister Claudette, probably because she's a real activist. They want to have nothing to do with breaking the law or with being arrested, so Sister Claudette is fuming, and some days I really WISH WISH WISH she would act more like a nun. She simply is not good at keeping her emotions under control, and I feel like saying to her, how the heck did you get to be thirty-five, acting like that? On the other hand, I get mad, too, because these beetleheaded St. Ursula's members are not exactly rising to the challenges confronting us. (What is their excuse? "It's summer!") It was so wonderful when I used to dream about the group. I could picture these orderly and powerful meetings, and I almost feel like canceling everything and taking the idea back. But what would I do with it?

I am trying harder and harder to keep an image of a healthy baby floating around in my head, along with all the nuclear paraphernalia. I like to think of myself as Psyche with a bosom full of fish but I'm really more like Ares, walking with Terror, Trouble, and Panic by my side.

* *

The mountain laurel and honeysuckle were blooming. Al and Raine were sitting on a bench in Central Park under a horse chestnut tree. "Hanging around the house isn't really good for me," Raine said.

"Graduation was a very sad event without you," he said.

"I know, but once Alice followed the white rabbit down the rabbit hole, there was no way to get back up. The real problem was that I could never picture myself in a cap and gown."

"The real problem was that you didn't go to school," he said.

She was smoothing her hands over her pregnant belly. "Did Frieda come back?" she said.

"No, and I don't think she will."

"Maybe she'll get disgusted with all the biking and weight-lifting and start longing for a couch potato like you."

He wished she would not talk about him with such frankness. "My psychiatrist said that Frieda and I are poorly suited to each other," he said. "That I met her when I was in a state of shock and grief over my grandmother's death, and she was very soothing. I wasted no time proposing. I thought nothing of spending half my week's salary on flowers, and then barely having the money to eat."

"I think that's romantic. Pavel never really gave up anything for me, or went out of his way very much. Now that he's gone, I have these big clumps of reality that thwomp into my head, usually in the middle of the night. He was someone I believed in. When he left me, he knew what he was doing, and he *chose* to do it. That's not very rabbinical, in my opinion."

"I guess he was scared," he said.

"Is love a careful thing, or does it just occur to us some-time down the road that we should have been more careful?"

"Don't ask me. I know very little about love. I call Frieda sometimes, but I know she can't wait to hang up and get back to *him*."

"It must be fun to run off with somebody."

"I wouldn't know."

"Let's run off together!" she said. She pushed herself up off the bench. "We can move to your farm. Yes, it's a great idea. Mary can come. It would be so superb—the baby would be born with the frogs and the birds singing all around him." He laughed when she started hopping around on the sidewalk, saying, *"Rivet! Rivet! Rivet!"* She sat back down and said, "Pavel and I used to try to have four brilliant thoughts every month—and this is definitely one of them."

"Can't you just see it?" he said. 'St. Ursula's Guidance Counselor Moves to Farm with Pregnant St. Ursula's Student.'"

"This paleontologist I know says the more risks you take, the more the odds will hold true. I think living on the farm would be kind of nice. Just for the summer."

"You're not serious, are you?"

"You have your St. Ursula's salary to live on, and Mary and I can clean people's houses."

"It's a depressed area. People clean their own houses."

"It doesn't matter. It's a fabulous idea, and your obstructions are meaningless. We can't be afraid of every little thing. We have a baby to think of now."

"*We?*" he said.

"My friends and I. What do you say, Al?"

"Although it's one of the most brilliant and innovative ideas I've ever heard, the answer is *no*. Not in ten million years."

"Okay—*not* in ten million years—next Monday. That'll give us a week to pack, and a week for me to talk Mary into it. I'll have to be really seductive because it's impossible to get Mary to do anything she doesn't feel like doing."

"It's impossible to get me to do something I don't feel like doing, too," he said.

"But you *do* want to. You just don't know it. You're one of these people with cold feet who's very hesitant when it comes to change and adventure. But that's okay. Mary will be our fearless leader."

"Oh, you mean Mary? Who doesn't even know about it?"

"Listen, Al. I don't think I can live with my parents anymore. And I think life on your farm would be fun. It would be a breathing space between catastrophes."

"Raine?" he said.

"Yes?"

"The answer is *no*."

* *

Spring has sprung—and so have I! I wear one of Mary's muumuus as camouflage, not because I'm embarrassed that every person in the street knows I had sex last November, but because I am truly tired of being stared at. I think it is so rude, and I often speak to people about their antediluvian manners, but for some reason, that only makes me madder. I like to go to the park, where the trees themselves are exotic and do not care in the least that I am a variant teenager. Janey comes over and rubs my back and tells me how lucky I am and says she wishes she was having a baby, too. It's sweet of her to say that even though it isn't true. Her mother gave me a present of three tiny pastel bibs with flowers embroidered on them, and when I opened the box, I cried. She said I'm courageous, but I don't feel very courageous. Kerunda says the great thing about a pregnancy is that it's a circle and all possibilities are open. No one point stands out more than any other point. Kerunda and Janey have nice ways of looking at everything, and I really feel lucky to have them in my life.

What type of a mother will I be? I think I have to make a choice. A, B, or C. (Vikey, Raisa, or Kerunda.) Kerunda changed her name from Eleanor as a way of inventing her own life. Vikey was enthusiastic about motherhood, I think, but I guess she was intimidated by Mother's cold talent, and they never really got along. Kerunda seems more like a friend than a mother to Janey, and I sense that sometimes Janey doesn't like this. I definitely want to have a wholesome relationship with my child, so I must try to be very friendly but not too friendly and very stern but not too stern. I want us to get along like Vikey and I did—but is it possible Homo sapiens has to skip a generation to enjoy that kind of delicious harmony?

Mary refuses to let me complain. She has this buck-up look in her eye, and I know from seventeen years of living with her that she thinks obstacles are an invitation to be brave and not an invitation to whine and complain. Mother and Daddy do not accept complaints either—they give me their you-made-your-own-bed-now-lie-in-it look, and I think, Did you haul that emaciated cliché all the way over from Slovakia? You should have left it there! I feel like I'm living in a house with an oil painting of Raisa and an oil painting of Karel on the wall, and every once in a while, they let fly some hostile remark, then melt back into the painting. I could stand there talking to the paintings all day and get no response—but when they feel like it, they speak. It seems quite possible that Lamont will become a father someday, and I CANNOT imagine treating him like this. But Mary would construe that comment as a complaint. I love being in the park, where it's so beautiful with the wild roses blooming, and when I'm lying in the pink crab apple petals fallen under the trees, I can only imagine happy endings to all stories.

* *

Al dreamed of meeting Frieda in the Mayflower Hotel and inviting her to quit her job and move to the farm with him. They could get some chickens and a few sheep, buy a pickup truck, grow flowers, attend church suppers, and plant potatoes, rosemary, and mustard greens in his grandmother's old vegetable garden. But if he called her, he was afraid she'd say something hurtful like, "I've never loved you, Alvin. Now that I've met Daniel, I realize what it's really like to be with a man, to live together and share everything. You were always so withdrawn, so lost in yourself."

And he wasn't sure he wanted her back. Day after day, he tried to find the courage to telephone her at work, but when he finally did pick up the phone, he decided to call Raine instead.

"Raine?" he said when she answered the phone, "Hi. Your idea isn't such a bad one after all."

"What idea?"

"You can come to the farm if you want."

"Since when?" she said.

"I've been thinking about it. I've decided to move up there myself, and I've also decided I should offer people what they need instead of what I feel like giving them. It's not a completely altruistic gesture. I don't know if I want to live alone in such a lonely place, but I have to get out of this apartment. All I can think about when I'm here is everything I wish I had done differently."

"Mother's always saying I should go out and rub my little wits together in the real world," Raine said.

"There's plenty of room for you on the farm. Come at least until the baby's born."

"That would be absolutely *great*, Al."

"Maybe your parents need some time to accept your predicament. I'm glad you had the idea, Raine. I know the house would feel lonely to me. We can keep each other company. We'll fry up some burdock like my grandmother used to do. What do you think?"

"Are you sure you want me to come?"

"Yes. I'm sure. It doesn't matter what people think, or even what Frieda thinks."

"Okay," she said. "So when is all this happening?"

"Next Saturday. Take the twelve o'clock train from Grand Central to Poughkeepsie, and get off at Cold Spring. I'll be at the station. Don't bring your bagpipes!"

He hung up and paced for a while in his hot, musty den, thinking, *Have you gone berserk? Are you out of your mind?*

* *

Al could still feel his grandmother's presence inside the farmhouse. Hanging on a peg in the kitchen was the clog almanac marked with feast days and cycles of the moon. The old rooms smelled of oilcloth and mildew. In the 1940s, his great-grandmother had planted the pine trees around the barn. Everything reminded him of his grandmother: the creaking floorboards, the steep staircase, the bubbled glass, the old Kalamazoo cookstove, the birds stenciled on the kitchen walls.

He imagined a dreamy woman painting the birds on the plaster, maybe a young pregnant woman like Raine. His relatives had lived here—people who had dreams and desires, caught up in the world of birth, life, marriage, death. In the big bed upstairs, a baby had been born, had created another life, and had one day sunk lifeless into the feathers. Sunlight streamed through the windows, as it had in his boyhood, onto the blue jug on the counter, the pine floors, the brass crucifix, the wallpaper of faded pink hollyhocks.

His grandmother disliked expressions of affection or emotion, but when Al visited her as a child, he loved to capture her in her chair, close his eyes, smell the scent of starch in her dress, feel his arms around her. Her eyes were a gentle honey color, and she moved through the rooms, big and soft and silent in her flowered dress and sweater, her shadow passing over him, the sun warming the back of his hair as he played on the floor by the window. She canned fruit. She shelled beechnuts. She snapped wax beans. These were her sounds. In her medicine basket, she kept thick violet syrup for his coughs, cedar leaves for her rheumatism, hog's fennel for their toothaches. As they worked on the farm, feeding the animals and cleaning their stalls, they listened to bullfrogs croaking, owls hooting, crickets and woodcocks singing in the grass. She said it was good luck to find brown crickets hiding in the house.

Food in those days was grown with the hands and harvested with the hands: peppers and garlic strung up in the kitchen, potatoes and squash and turnips kept in the root cellar, parsnips stored under the snow. His grandmother cut noodles and draped them over the chairs to dry, she drew puffy golden loaves of bread out of the huge black woodstove. She taught him how to get the fire hotter with piffy wood and how to cool it down with green wood.

The mockingbirds had grown quiet and secretive. The starlings' speckles were fading. The daisies and day lilies were in bloom, and the roses, and the blue chicory at the sides of the road. He sat in the pine needles by the barn as fog settled down over the blue mountains and birds circled the sky, grackles with a purple sheen, baby sparrows flying like big, soft moths. The black eye of a nuthatch glittered in its white face. In the thickets surrounding the house were kingfishers, rusty blackbirds, blue jays, sparrows, black-capped chickadees. He sat and listened to their soft chattering.

The only games his grandmother had played with him were ones that coincided with her chores. On a hot summer day, he'd lie down in the garden, and she'd water him with the hose, and he would close his eyes as the water soaked into him, and she'd laugh, and he'd lie there grinning, getting wetter and wetter, feeling utterly happy and at peace.

* *

He carried Raine's two duffel bags up the hill to the farm's rusty mailbox, then they turned in to the pasture, walked down the hill to the farmhouse, and climbed up onto the old porch.

"Wow," she said. "This place is decrepit."

"I see you brought your bagpipes."

She smiled. "I thought you might need some cheering up."

He gave her a tour of the house, then they sat at the kitchen table. Raine looked around. The kitchen seemed very old-fashioned. She imagined Al's grandmother cooking over the six-burner woodstove. There was a porcelain stove as well, a rust-stained sink, glass cupboards filled with flowered plates and cups, and chairs and a small table covered with oilcloth. A clothesline still ran from the porch to a redbud tree in the yard.

"Look at all the tweety-birds!" she said.

"I'd love some of Frieda's sauerbraten right about now," he said.

"Or some of Mary's lentil soup."

"Or Frieda's apple klosse."

"Or Mary's cornbread."

"Or Frieda's beef Wellington," he said, laughing.

"It feels safe here. I never feel completely safe in the city. People always want something from me." She looked at him. "Everybody except you."

"Except me?" He got up to clear the dishes, then he turned back to her and said, "I did an awful thing, Raine."

"What kind of awful thing?"

"Something really inappropriate that I should have told you about before you came up here. But I was too afraid." He paused. "Remember the day you left your books in my office? I read your journal. I was curious about you. It was a very confusing time for me. I could feel my life about to fall apart—not that that's any excuse. I'm sorry, Raine. I'm glad I told you. It feels much better to confess."

"I think confession is a rip-off. First we give someone power over us, and then we confess stuff that's really none of their business. Did I write anything interesting? Did I embarrass myself?"

"No—of course not," he said. "I'm really sorry Raine."

"It's okay, Al."

He wished she had not so easily forgiven him.

"My father says the universe is younger than a lot of stars," she said. "Life feels like that sometimes—like here we are stuck out on this farm. Once you were married and I was a student at St. Ursula's. Now we're living here. I'm about to be a mother, and you're about to get divorced. We're stars without a universe."

"Yes," he said. "Wouldn't you think if I really loved Frieda, I'd spend my time thinking about how happy she is with Daniel? How happy they both are?"

"What *do* you think about?"

"Nothing in particular," he said, although he was continually picturing Frieda curled up on Daniel's waterbed.

"Maybe you should be happy for Frieda, and maybe if Mary goes back to Greenland, I should be happy for her."

"Why should you be happy when your worst fear comes true? You love Mary, and love endures. Remember what St. Paul said? 'Love is patient and kind; love is not jealous or boastful; it is not arrogant or rude. Love does not insist on its own way; it is not irritable or resentful; it does not rejoice at wrong, but rejoices in the right. Love bears all things, believes all things, hopes all things, endures all things.'"

"That doesn't sound like any love I ever heard of," she said.

He laughed and said, "Me either."

* *

I am now an employee at a shop called Animal Crackers. The Talmud says that one must learn a trade and not become a burden to the community. Al is against my working, but I did not want to sponge off him for everything, so I am working Wednesday to Saturday, from ten to six.

They made me promise I'd continue to work after Lamont is born. (They must be desperate for employees.) I'm hoping they'll let me keep him in a basket out of the way where the peach-faced lovebirds can tweet to him while I work. So here I am, passing out parakeets to the lonely and bereft, and trying to reassure the turtles and parrots and goldfish no one buys that they really are beautiful. I feel like saying to my customers, "Get your life together—don't use a bird to make you happy!" But I remain silent because I need this job, and it seems to me that what being an adult entails is learning to curb your most authentic impulses and slowly becoming ersatz. "It seems really horrible to be selling animals," I said to Al, but he claims there wouldn't be any finches in the Northeast if three house finches hadn't escaped from a pet shop in 1941. I think he made that up to make me feel better, but he swears it's true. And Al does know his birds.

But do these birds really want to spend their summer incarcerated in cages? Wouldn't they rather be sitting in the tops of trees, eating nutmeg? When no one is around, and my boss Mr. Chutter is upstairs, I actually talk to them. When Mr. Chutter was out with the flu—oh, what a relief!—I opened all the cage doors at the end of my shift. But I'm sure freedom is a dangerous thing in the animal world. Fruity the parakeet was the only one to fly out.

Oh my gosh—I catch a view of myself in the mirror

and cannot believe I have any connection with the image that appears in the glass. I look like a pear tree with a tumor! It is very, very odd going around like this, getting on the train and everyone scattering, people offering me seats and looking at me out of the sides of their eyes, like the parakeets at work, sizing me up in their peripheral vision but refusing to look me straight in the eye. Occasionally, I take my clothes off and look at myself in the mirror and try to think of myself as some kind of madonna.

Most of the time, I'm terrified of childbirth, but Mary says it's a very serene (if painful) event. The baby will be born here on the farm (she claims), the midwife will come, I'll be squatting on the floor, Mary will place rocks in a circle around me, and she'll sing her Greenlandic birth songs. "Are you sure that all sounds okay?" I asked her, tending to think I better go find a hospital that smells of antiseptics instead of seaweed and ravens' feet. But Mary is quite insistent and headstrong when it comes to matters of life and death. Al says don't be ridiculous, of course I'm going to a hospital, but he prefers not to talk about it. He doesn't want to think about where babies come from. He is definitely NOT the person I am going to count on when the big day arrives. I'm nervous, but part of me can't wait to see this amazing tiny creature of my own making. It's hard for me to admit that Pavel is at all involved in this project. How could I have been so wrong about anybody? The night I had *dinner at his house, I should have said, "Pavel, why did you plop that black witch's wig on my head and take my picture?" But instead I said to him and his mother, "Thank you so much for the wonderful dinner." What was wonderful about it? It was more like the primeval banquet where the pious ate the sea monster Leviathan, the beast Behemoth, and the huge bird Ziz.*

My first discussion with Lamont will be about his father, and how I thought he had grandmotherly impulses and would be willing to rescue Jews in Slovakia, but instead when he had a chance to meet a new and interesting Jew — his own son — he hopped aboard a fast flight to Israel. (I never saw one scrap of the baby wardrobe he promised to buy for Lamont.) Yet telling my child the truth about his father is probably quite cruel — so what is the solution? To lie to my own son? Molly the midwife has a little office in the village, and I go there to have my blood pressure taken. I guess I am in excellent health and have nothing to worry about — just PAVEL PAVEL PAVEL and PAIN PAIN PAIN.

* *

"I'll get Frieda back for you," Raine said as she arranged a bunch of wildflowers in a vase.

He wished she'd sit down. Her face was pale. Her belly was huge.

The two of them seemed to get through the days by

pretending they were living a normal life, but occasionally he envisioned them careening ahead, inevitably, into their unimaginable destinies. He and Frieda divorced. Raine with a baby. What if the baby were born deformed? What if it were sick? Even if it were healthy, who was going to take care of it? Raine showed no signs of becoming more maternal. What would life as a single man be like? Would he actually start dating? Would Raine start bringing home women for him?

She put the vase down on the table and said, "I don't think getting her back will be that hard."

"You are not to go near Frieda."

"Why not? I hate to see you so miserable, Al. I think you and Frieda need each other. If only we could get that stupid manling out of the way. It's horrible to think that someone of my generation is hanging his hat on Frieda's bedpost."

Al was buttering his toast. "Raine, it's my problem. Okay?"

"But with friends is there such a thing as *my* problem and *your* problem? Look at the way you took me in. You take really good care of me. You won't let me give you rent. You won't even let me pay for groceries."

"I'm happy to help if I can, but I would sincerely appreciate it if you would not reciprocate."

"You should see yourself. You have such a hangdog

look. What are you going to do when you have to face all those St. Ursula's girls in September?"

"I'm hoping to spend the summer resting up and changing gears."

"But I really feel like helping you," she said.

"I don't *want* your help."

"I know you're just saying that because you're out of ideas. You don't have a clue how to get Frieda back because you don't understand women."

"Frieda isn't coming back, Raine. I'm beginning to accept that."

"What if she still loves you? Maybe she's under Daniel's spell. He could be one of those cult leader types. Do you think we should formulate a rescue plan?"

"I want you to promise me you'll stay out of it. Mess up your own life if you want, but stay out of mine."

"*E pluribus unum*," she said.

* *

Frieda had the amazing beauty, the enigmatic smile, and the unbridled energy of someone who was trying to stifle her happiness, a woman whose desire to return to her young lover was in conflict with her wish to be kind.

The dining room of the Mayflower Hotel was glimmering with silver and crystal and seemed like the perfect place for couples to meet for cocktails before going upstairs to a bucket of champagne and the lush privacy of their own room.

"I'm sure this is the wrong place for us to be meeting," Frieda said, pouring their coffee out of a silver pot. At a table by the window, years earlier, Al had arranged for a tall waiter with curly black hair to serve Frieda a lemon tart with his grandmother's opal engagement ring implanted in the center of it. Frieda had smiled, licked the whipped cream off the ring, and slipped it onto her finger. It was the happiest day of his life.

"But you insisted we come here," she said.

"Sometimes I think men *should* be insistent. That's what women expect. Remember when you used to hate biking? And Daniel insisted you try it...."

"I got your letter," Frieda said.

"What letter?"

"That beautiful letter you wrote. Thank you."

"What beautiful letter?" he said.

"The one you sent me. I cried when I got it. It was so poignant. And so honest."

"You think so?" he said.

"Yes I do. I never realized you thought all those things."

"I didn't either," he said.

"I've never known you to be so expressive. I'm not sure I even knew you still loved me. I never imagined you could be *that* romantic."

He sat silently, tapping his spoon on the linen napkin. "Then I guess it's good we're apart," he said. "Because I'm really not romantic and I never will be. I'm too selfish and too pragmatic. I imagine Daniel is romantic."

"He's certainly appreciative. And attentive."

"I don't want you to come back to me because of a sales pitch, Frieda."

"You're thinking I'm coming back?"

"If you ever do, it should be because of what I represent, of our history, of who I am and who I'm becoming. Anyone can write a romantic letter. It's a form of schmoozing. But not everyone can look deeply into another person and see beauty there, and honor it, and want more of it. That letter was *not* romantic. I didn't even write it. Raine did. She has this idea that she can lure you back."

"You mean—"

"I told her not to. But she's a very imperious and perverse young woman."

"I find it hard to believe that a teenager could write a letter like that."

"She's very smart when she's using her intelligence," he said. "Which is rarely."

Frieda was drumming her polished fingernails on the table. He was tapping his foot against the chair. "You and I never talked about anything scary," she said. "We'd argue and then retreat, but Daniel is teaching me to share feelings until the conflict dissolves and the relationship grows deeper through a new understanding of the other person."

"So—you've had your first fight," he said, pleased to observe a chink in the armor.

"Daniel doesn't keep a Pearl Harbor file, like you did."

"I respected you too much to yell at you. Is that what you mean?"

"Daniel taught me that it isn't respectful to withhold feelings. Feelings are meant to be shared. We show a lack of trust in others and in the relationship when we shy away from anger."

"Everyone has a secret garden, Frieda, but it's not surprising you never told me about your affair. You never told me anything. And I never told you much of anything either. The dialogue between a knight and his lady is really a monologue."

"You're entitled to your view of the world, and I'm entitled to mine."

"But that isn't what marriage is supposed to be."

"Why didn't you want children?" she asked.

"Children are like mice. You let one in, and a whole bunch come running in after them. I haven't had a good night's sleep since Raine's baby was born."

"You do look tired, Al."

"And you look very well rested."

"Yes," she said. "I feel relieved. I guess I feel almost grateful to Raine. She's only a teenager, but she seems to know how to handle your morose streak."

"What morose streak?" he said.

"I'm sorry—I shouldn't have said that. Is the baby cute?"

"I don't know," he said. "I guess so. She named him after me."

"You're *kidding*."

"And Mary's mother. His name is Alvin Juulut Gandhi Rassaby. He arrived three weeks early. We call him Alvy." Al imagined receiving a pastel letter in the mail, addressed to *Mr. Alvin Klepatar* in Frieda's curving script. Seeing the envelope in his mailbox, he would think it was a love letter; then he would slide out the card and discover it was an announcement of the birth of Frieda and Daniel's baby.

"Well, I'm glad you're finally happy," she said.

"Who said I'm happy?" he said, remembering Frieda as a bride, her lace veil, her breasts swelling up out of scallops of ecru. "It's impossible to be happy with an infant in the house. It doesn't matter, though, because Raine's moving out soon."

"I'm glad you think so," she said.

"She's falling into her old habits. Two weeks after the baby was born, off she went to her infernal bomb group. She either leaves the little one behind or drags him along in a corduroy pouch that I was forced to buy since I found her carrying him around in a pail. She's sneaky as hell. She never tells me what she's up to. I'm the one who has to go down and bail her out when she gets arrested for demonstrating."

"You're in love with her, aren't you?" Frieda said, smoothing her hands over the tablecloth. He hated to see the familiar hand without its wedding ring.

Al wasn't sure how to respond. He remembered saying to the psychiatrist after his arrest, *I don't really want to think about what these feelings are telling me about my own moral code.*

Do you have any plans to sleep with her? the doctor asked.

Of course I don't, but I'm afraid I do.

Fantasies, you mean? But no real intentions?

No, he said. *The thought is abhorrent to me. She's a nice kid. I'd like to help her. I'd never want to hurt her. I can't say I desire her. It's more a feverish need to protect her. I worry about her all the time.*

"If you mean, do I want to sleep with Raine, the answer is no," he said. "But I *do* want to sleep. If the baby isn't crying and keeping me awake, I'm lying there, worrying that he'll die of SIDS. I keep getting up to see if he's still breathing."

"You've never had a penchant for giving. And suddenly you're doing all this for her?"

"I wish you wouldn't sound so suspicious."

Frieda was tapping a sugar lump with her spoon, trying to get it to melt in her cold coffee.

"Do you see any patterns here?" she asked.

"What kind of patterns?"

"Of people who go off and leave babies. First your father left you, then your mother left you, now Raine is leaving her baby. It's a pattern you're apparently attracted to. She goes off and leaves a helpless infant behind."

"Some of these anti-nuclear activists have been sentenced to ten years in prison. The mouthy ones."

"I'd love to meet the baby. Would you mind if we biked up on Saturday?"

"Who's we?" he said.

"Daniel and I."

"*You* can bike up if you want."

"Al, this is a time of transition for me, too. It isn't easy. I'm trying to be upbeat. I'm trying to keep the peace between us."

"There isn't any peace between us, Frieda. None. Zip. Bagatelle. *Peace?* I hate pretending there is."

"There isn't, but there could be," she said. She looked as though she were about to cry.

He stared down at the tablecloth and saw his reflection pinched into a silver spoon. "You left me without saying a word," he said.

"I wrote you a long letter."

"I couldn't read it," he said.

"Why not?"

"For the same reason I can't throw myself on my own sword. You should have talked to me. You should have asked me to change. You should have suggested a marriage counselor...."

He watched her bite into her cake. Frieda had had everything as a child. An orthodontist. A pediatrician. A bicycle. A country club. Parents. "Frieda, listen to me," he said. "We created a home together, and the purpose of a home is to protect us from the dangerous fluctuations of the physical world. From unwelcome attention from predators and parasites."

He wanted to do something drastic to gain her back, to tumble and flash and sing some rich complex melody that only she would recognize.

"So you think you'll marry her?" Frieda said.

"Who?"

"Raine."

"Are you out of your mind? Raine's a friend. You didn't even bother to acknowledge our fifteenth anniversary, but Raine baked me an anniversary cake, and you know what? It had *black* icing. She made it out of sugar and soy sauce."

"I think it was manipulative of her to name the baby after you," she said.

"You're a very suspicious person, aren't you? I never realized it until this moment. My grandmother was, too. She was always looking for people's ulterior motives. You think the worst of everybody—you wonder what they want. But guess what, Frieda? Friends don't want anything."

"I'm sure she wants something."

"She has an insatiable desire to contribute to the progress of civilization," he said. "Who knows why?"

"You fell in love with her, Al."

"I'll admit, I fell someplace. And who knows where I'll end up."

A man who fought in armor for hours, or spent two years going to Jerusalem for the good of his soul, was able in all seriousness to kneel before his lady and thank her for having made him a better knight and Christian by causing him suffering and rarely fulfilled desire. But did he really want moral and ethical improvement to become the only benefit of love? Did he want to be a man whose melancholy was a source of happiness and whose only reward was yearning?

* *

So many secrets are kept from children, and birth is one of them. (Death is another.) My expectations for the birth were that there would be pain like the shooting pains I get in my side when I run after I eat, but the pain was more like getting run over by a train, and then the train speeding off, and you go, "Thank God"—and then a minute later, you get run over by another train. Who exactly devised this particular route for the survival of the species? On top of that,

I have never seen Mary acting stranger. I think she took all her anxiety about me having the baby three weeks early (or having the baby at all) by lugging rocks up the stairs and making a circle with them in the master bedroom (which Al was kind enough to give to me). Then Mary invited all her ancestors into the room and plopped feathers and ravens' feet all around, and chunks of whalebone, and Molly arrived and my primary impulse (if we had a phone) would have been to call 911. Suddenly, I was suspicious of Mary's advice. Is this what becoming an adult is like? I have heard Mary's stories for years and I always loved them, but I did not appreciate the encroachment of the ancestors at the very moment I was becoming a mother and was about to be whooshed into another form. With all the ancestors there, I was afraid I could end up changed—possibly into a bear giving birth to a baby bear—and then I would be in a fix: namely, unable to talk and primarily interested in blueberries and salmon. "Mary, will you tone it down?" I said, but she wouldn't, and Molly seemed unruffled by Mary's intensely northern inklings. I had always been the weird one, and it was strange to suddenly be the normal one surrounded by kooks—with all the kooks' attention focused on me. Then add to all that emotional perplexity, this unbelievable pain! Well, Al (representing relative normality) had made himself scarce, so I had no choice but to plunge into this rather bizarre experience with whatever depleted energy

I had. Something rambunctious had crept out of Mary, and it was quite extraordinary—I don't think I've ever seen it before. For the birth itself, I awarded myself a C+—babyish and irritable a lot of the time but generally coping and at times even brave. And there's such a happy ending! The baby appeared, and he was this beautiful creature who looked as though he had been folded up too long but would soon unfold and become this phenomenal baby-human whose name could not possibly be Lamont. The pain suddenly became rather inconsequential—maybe that's why nobody ever talks about it.

I am trying very hard to feel sorry for my parents because they didn't want me and they don't want Alvy, and although I sent Mary back home with a ton of pictures, they have never actually seen my baby in person. I've called them from the pay phone in the village, and as I dial, my brainwaves are going bang-clash-whop, and my heart is skipping beats. But Karel and Raisa are screening their calls, and it's true that they can't call me back because Al is dragging his feet getting a phone installed in the house. (Maybe he's afraid Frieda will phone requesting a divorce.) Still, wouldn't you think my parents would just show up with their arms full of baby presents? They would discover that Alvy is absolutely fabulous, in spite of his rather dubious parentage. Didn't Stalin have a daughter who went to Africa to help starving children? I think it's quite possible for a sleaze to

give birth to an innocent. For God's sake, Karel and Raisa,
take an empathy pill!

* *

Sitting by the bedroom window after midnight, with strips of moonlight shining in on the pine floor, they were taking turns rocking the baby's cradle. Raine was playing Scrabble with herself.

"Sometimes I couldn't imagine what Frieda was thinking," Al said. "Part of me was attracted to the mystery because I've always loved reading about the troubadours. It's sort of a hobby of mine. I liked the way the troubadour was energized and lifted to new spiritual heights by his devotion to a married woman. But in this case, the married woman was my wife."

"That's kind of freaky, Al."

"Some things are freaky, but you get used to them, and they begin to seem normal. Since there are just two people living in isolation, normality in a marriage can get very, *very* abnormal. You wake up one morning and find a stranger in the bed, but the stranger isn't your spouse. It's you."

"You make marriage sound very tantalizing."

"Frieda telling me about her affair was like having my hair set on fire. I never realized she could be deliberately cruel and then could sugar-coat it with concern for me, as though she were telling me for my own good. It's one of the things I don't understand about organized religion. So many people like Frieda trot off to their place of worship, then turn around and feel perfectly comfortable doing something cruel for somebody else's own good."

"You think that's religion's fault?" she said, studying the letters on the Scrabble board.

"I think religion and humanity have a weird relationship. I was amazed when Frieda—the good Catholic—left me and moved in with Daniel. I've always been jealous and insecure, and I half-thought I was imagining the feelings between them. I was so out-of-touch with her, I had no idea what was real and what wasn't."

"Reality's always been a problem for me, too," Raine said.

"And here we are with this baby looking up to us—but neither of us knows who we are."

"Maybe we should start with who we'd like to be. I guess you have to imagine something before you can make it real."

"I'd like to be more compassionate," Al said.

"I'd like to be *less* compassionate. There's a really blurry line between me and other people. There's very little border patrol. Mary says she admires me because I went out on a limb, and I returned. But I don't know if I *did* return. What I'd really like is for Karel and Raisa to be proud of me."

"If you were my daughter, I'd be proud of you," he said.

"The way you had this baby, with very little encouragement from anyone, and the way you grapple with things. You don't let yourself off the hook like I do."

"I think you've handled the separation from Frieda very courageously."

"By stealing a bunch of groceries and an eighty-dollar slip?"

"By being nice to another person—in this case, me. Instead of thinking of your reputation, or of what you wanted, you thought of me. I think it's really important to be there for someone when it costs you something."

She wanted to remain strong. She wanted to be like Moses' sister Miriam, who was a source of sustenance to her people. As a bat mitzvah, wasn't she obliged to fulfill the commandments? Wasn't she supposed to develop the clarity of her voice? Hadn't she sung the song that the Israelites sang crossing the Red Sea? Hadn't she chanted the ancient melodies of the Haftarah?

* *

It was a world of vivid colors and floral imaginings. A girl in a pink ballerina dress came walking down the hillside with her arms full of flowers. I thought it was an Irish fairy. Thousand of red roses were bobbing toward me as I was sitting by the window, nursing Alvy and realizing that the farm is an awfully strange place. It seems like anything could happen here, and it did—because the flowers were from

Mrs. Orzagh! I was amazed, but the flowers were just a prelude to a surprise party planned for Alvy by Mrs. O. and Mother and Daddy. (All along, they were just pretending to be mean.) They paraded into the house, lugging shopping bags from Bloomingdale's that were full of presents for my adorable boy, as well as a letter of apology postmarked from Israel. It said, "Dearest Raine—I'm sorry I acted so badly toward you. I treated you like a thing without feelings and will always feel absolutely awful about my sociopathic callousness. I am not asking you to forgive me. I am only saying I'm sorry. How can I be a rabbi, exhorting people to be their best selves, when I stepped on you like you were a worthless ant? I can't wait to meet the baby. My mother wants you two and Al to move in with her. I will be home for Rosh Hashanah and Yom Kippur and will be making amends at that time. I plan to walk on my knees from the airport to Al's farm and even then, I won't have begun to demonstrate my sorrow for treating you in such a hardhearted, coldblooded, cruel, and detached manner. You are the only woman I will ever love. Pavel."

"Alvy, you have grandparents," I said, and they ferried him off in their fat and thin arms as Al came downstairs from his nap and thought he was imagining the sight of Mrs. Orzagh standing at the stove, cooking bryndzove halusky, and Raisa sitting with Alvy on her lap, gazing down at him like he was a Stradivarius. It was decided that we will go

home for dinner every Sunday and that Al will come too,
since Mother and Daddy feel undying gratitude toward him
for taking such good care of us. Now, everything is fine,
wonderful, fabulous, and glorious.

* *

Turning the corner on West 88th Street, Raine slowed her pace as she approached the wrought-iron gate. She picked Alvy some phlox from the garden, then pressed her face against the glass of the French door. Mary was kneading dough on the counter. She looked up, hurried to the door, unbolted the four locks, and burst out laughing when Raine came in with the baby.

"Any sign of *los parentos*?" Raine said.

"No, no. They're gone. Oh, look at that sweetie! He's grown."

Raine handed the baby to her and said, "They've been asking about me, right?"

"Right," Mary said.

"Swear on a Bible, Mary."

"Are you calling me a liar?"

"Yes. Greenlanders think it's polite to say what people want to hear. But it isn't good for people to hear what they want to hear. It's good for us to hear the *truth*."

"Your parents are angry," Mary said, looking down.

"About what?"

"I don't know."

"Well?"

"They don't like you living on that farm."

"What else?"

"They don't like Al. They call him swine."

"Swine? Pavel's the swine!"

Mary rocked the baby and said, "They think Pavel's swine, too."

"Did you show them the pictures of Alvy?" Raine said.

"They think he's darling."

"The truth!"

Mary looked down at the baby for a while. "They couldn't bring themselves to look at the pictures," she said.

"Do they want Alvy just to vanish?"

"The world softens little by little," Mary said. "But it takes time."

"But look at him. He's getting teeth. Pretty soon he'll need dentures."

Mary laughed and said, "He's too little for teeth."

"Well, there's nothing even slightly grandparenty on the Pavel end. I've been waiting for Mrs. Orzagh to send me a dozen roses, but so far they haven't arrived. That's because she has taken the position of defending Pavel. It's really disgusting. Love should have some limits. I'm sure Mrs. Hitler thought little Adolf was adorable too."

"I think he's hungry," Mary said, handing the baby back to her.

Raine settled into the chair by the window to nurse him and said, "Guess what, Mary? I want you to be Alvy's father."

"Me?"

"Yes. You'd be a great father. I don't want gender issues to stand in the way."

"No, no, Raine. Alvy's father must be a man."

"But you'd be the perfect father."

"What about Al?"

"Al hates babies, and children irritate him. I try to look at it as one of his quirks. So Alvy has no father, no grandparents, no great-grandparents, and even Al is acting rather peculiar. He seems to dislike Sister Claudette, and he has no faith whatsoever in the potential of St. Ursula's Girls Against the Atomic Bomb to make the world a safer place. To tell you the truth, I don't think he ever did."

"Did you see any of your friends from the street?" Mary asked.

"I haven't seen anyone since I became a hausfrau. Did you tell them I had the baby?"

"Yes. They were happy."

"How does this place feel without me?" Raine said.

"It feels quiet and peaceful. And lonely."

Raine reached for Mary's hand. "It is absolutely splendiferous being a mother, Mary. I was afraid I'd have nothing left to give Alvy except this dried-up heart left over from the Pavel-pummeling. But I can't imagine loving anyone more. Al says that being betrayed hasn't hurt either of us permanently. He says it probably hurt Pavel and Frieda more, because neither of them bothered to apologize. Al has this confession-penance-forgiveness thing imprinted in his brain, but I have a different view of forgiveness and am not about to forgive Pavel for his reptilian manners."

Mary was amused by the faces Alvy was making. "Look at those tiny hands!" she said. "Doesn't he seem like an angel?"

Raine went out to the garden and climbed the tree. The chrysanthemums and black-eyed Susans were in bloom. She wanted to talk to the tree, as she always had, but the tree now seemed less a part of her and more a part of the garden. She pictured Pavel swinging like a monkey on a branch outside her room, but instead she wanted to envision Alvy climbing the tree, and his grandparents loving him. She wished she had simply closed the curtains and let Pavel hang there. She wished she had been colder and shrewder and smarter because now she knew for sure that the man she had loved with her whole heart did not even exist.

* *

Al hated the sound of the baby crying. He wished he could soothe him, but he rarely could. Still, he was spending more and more time with Alvy since Raine was often either working or going into the city for her bomb meetings. He was sure she would be sentenced to jail, the court designating him Alvy's permanent guardian, and he'd take custody of the baby reluctantly, as his grandmother had taken custody of him. Little Alvy would sense his hesitation because children know everything.

As he walked around the house with the baby, Al tried to reassure himself. Raine was naturally lucky, wasn't she? He wanted to believe that the shadows would snatch at her but never quite catch her.

"In two weeks, school starts, and I have to go back to work," he said to her one morning as she was nursing the baby in the living room. "Which means that you are going to have to *behave*, and that will mean giving up your job or finding childcare, parting company with your flamboyant girlfriend, Sister Claudette, and making some plans."

"I guess you're tired of taking care of Alvy," Raine said. "But I think he's been good for you. Otherwise, you'd be spending the summer moping around."

"Sometimes people need to mope around. It's part of the healing process."

"Are you going back to your old apartment?" she said.

"Frieda and I decided not to renew the lease. Daniel's renting a moving truck. He's planning to put his muscles to work, dismantling my life."

"You should have asked Frieda for alimony. She was the

one who ran off. She probably owes you something."

"You know what, Raine? You're the one who owes me something. Remember when we talked about you coming to the farm? And I said you could stay until the baby's born?"

"Yes."

"Well, Alvy's five weeks old."

"You mean you want us to leave?" she said.

Al put his hand on her shoulder and said, "No. I don't. I want you to show some responsibility, and some consideration for me."

"I think Alvy expects me to do more than stay home, don't you?"

"You think he expects *me* to stay home?" he said. "You can't give yourself to children halfway, Raine. It makes them feel pale and unworthy."

* *

Sometimes I wonder if the world would be very different if I didn't exist. On the one hand, there would be happy, tranquil lives for Mother and Daddy. On the other hand, Mary has been employed for seventeen years because of me, and I saved her from certain dangerous liaisons. I know I made Vikey happier because we were so much alike and no one understood her Jewish leanings, but I certainly did. I've probably been an impedimenta for Pavel, and then there's the nuclear stockpile to consider. Will my presence on earth make one tiny difference, or will the arsenals keep growing bigger, the more the merrier? Spending thirty-five billion dollars a year keeping our nuclear stockpile in good condition is in my opinion like keeping the showers working well at Auschwitz.

I'm sure I've made a difference to Alvy. He seems really thrilled to be here. "The descending knife can be halted in midair," it says in the Torah. Maybe he'll have children who will have children who will have children who will say, "Remember great-great-grandmother Raine? She was mentally ill and attracted to selfish religious egomaniacs, but she had some great ideas."

And then perhaps they will talk about my redeeming love, Russell Schweickart. Yesterday, when Al was watching the baby, I went into the city to see what Sister Claudette was up to and to TRY TRY TRY to push St. Ursula's Girls Against the Atomic Bomb into notoriety. After Sister Claudette and I ate lunch in her soup kitchen, we stopped in at the 42nd Street library and I found this unbelievable speech Russell Schweickart made in 1987, five years before I met him. I showed it to Sister Claudette, and she practically fainted. I was ecstatic the whole way home on the train. I can't wait to read it to Al and Alvy. It turns out that when he was young, before he became an astronaut, Russell was assigned to an F-100 squadron at an airbase in Taiwan, and every few weeks, he had to stand nuclear alert. Sometimes he'd lie on top of a nuclear bomb and look up at the sky and try to imagine what he would do if the call came to scramble the bombers. Here are his exact words:

Would I do it? That was the question I wanted to face; that was the purpose of the terrifying ritual I would go through, trying to face the reality of why I was there, and what my responsibility might be.

On what basis do I decide whether or not to release this nuclear weapon, knowing that hundreds of thousands of people would die as a result? I would look at the stars and search my soul for the moral basis on which I might decide. I was aware of the individual moral burden of an action that would kill people I would never see. And I was also aware of the complex system of which I was a part, a system whose purpose of preventing war through deterrence would be corrupted (and the world therefore endangered) should the possibility of my electing not to release the weapon be known. I knew I'd had very little knowledge, if any, of what was going on in the rest of the world. Was half of it already gone? What about my family? My hometown? I wouldn't know their fate. Even so, did these questions have any relevance to the decision I had to make? How can society function if, in the most critical situations, individuals claim for themselves the right to decide that which has already been decided by society as a whole?...

Years later... I realized with horror the poor quality

and incompleteness of the information on which I had to base such decisions. I began to understand how much human frailty and subjectivity were woven into the most critical decision-making. And after much agony I came to realize, knowing what I know now, that if I had to decide again, lying there under the stars, my back pressed against the bomb, I wouldn't drop it. My specific decision isn't the point—it's rather that as a young man I was unwilling to trust my own sense of rightness when facing a momentous moral dilemma. I now understand that we can't pass along such decisions to higher authority, for there is no higher authority than that which exists in each of us, individually, as we face our complicated and ambiguous world. In my view, it's these personal moral choices, when repeated and aggregated in the behavior of family, of communities, of nations, that are the very essence of our survival. Will we have the wisdom and courage to accept the individual moral authority within each of us? Or will we defer to experts and impersonal systems of authority in the false belief that in them reside greater wisdom and morality? In how we answer these questions may lie the outcome of the great experiment of life.

* *

Al was in an exceedingly bad mood. Who said babies were wonderful? Who said they were cute? Alvy was *not* cute. He was bald, clamorous, and selfish. Yet it wasn't only the baby that was bothersome to him but his reaction to him. Alvy made him feel like a cold fish. Al couldn't help being irritated after he changed him, fed him, cooed to him in a false but diligent way, then finally lowered him into the haven of his cradle. Within fifteen minutes, Alvy usually started to cry again, perhaps because a haven always implied a threat. The cry progressed from a whimper to a yap to a squawk to a yowl. Beyond the mechanics of changing the baby and feeding him, he had no notion of how to respond to someone so small and helpless.

"What do you want?" he'd demand of the tiny creature. He'd pluck him up and walk him around the house, but the baby was rarely soothed by his peregrinations. "You want your mother, don't you? You don't want me and I don't want you." He gingerly placed Alvy into Raine's pouch, buckled him to his chest and walked down the hill to look at the clump of sunflowers growing by the barn. "Your father's a Slovakian lunatic rabbi, and your mother's a dreamer nutcase who wants to be a heroine, and nothing in your life will ever be real," he said. He sat on the grass and looked down at the baby's imploring eyes. He was tired of people who wanted things from him but would not articulate what they were. If only the baby could say, "Feed me," "Rock me," "I'm tired," "My stomach hurts."

The sun crept over the ridgepole of the barn, leaving them in a pool of purple shade. A red-tailed hawk flew overhead. Empty chrysalises were dangling from sticky milkweed plants. The butterflies had escaped. The baby had finally fallen asleep, bored with Al's grumblings, and Raine was trekking through the pasture toward them, wearing her backpack. "You two look adorable!" she said, flinging herself down in the grass.

"I'm glad you think so," he said. "Where have you been?"

"I told you—I had a meeting in the city."

"No, you didn't tell me. You left me a note. Remember?"

"Thanks for watching the little angel," she said. "Sister Claudette—"

"Don't say *one* more word," he said.

"What's wrong, Al?"

"I didn't have time to weed the garden or replant the asparagus or go into town to do my errands."

"How come?" she said.

"Because your baby was wailing in my ear. He's not the little angel you think he is."

"What do you mean? Alvy never cries."

"He never cries when you're around. That's because you're his mother. He likes you. He doesn't like me. And I don't like him."

"You're just in one of your moods."

"That's right. I am. Because you remind me an awful

lot of my mother."

"Your mother?" she said. "Katy? The alcoholic?"

"Yes. That's what you two have in common: irresponsibility. And Sister Claudette is another one. She's luring you into civil disobedience. It's totally, one hundred percent irresponsible." He looked down at Alvy's toe popping out of his terrycloth suit. "This outfit you got for him at the thrift store is ripping," he added.

"I think it's really good we're working out our conflicts," she said.

"You were the one who chose to keep the baby. You were the one to pick Pavel, the flighty rabbi, as a mate. I was the one who decided not to have children. Remember? I moved to the farm so I could think about my life and reflect on the eternal questions."

"We can't just believe things, Al. We have to show that we believe them."

"Somehow Alvy knows he has only you," he said, looking down at the baby. "He feels forlorn and abandoned when you leave the house. Why can't you understand that?"

* *

Cold Spring would be a great place to start a chapter of St. Ursula's Girls Against the Atomic Bomb. People here might like the idea of ending our flirtation with the devil. Then Sister Claudette could take over the group in the city, Janey could have her group at college, and small satellite chapters would begin to cover the countryside like missile silos.

I love to put on my sunglasses and walk with Alvy through the village, pretending I'm Mrs. Gandhi carrying Mohandas through Porbandar. I want very much to be a responsible mother and I wonder if I should tape a subliminal message for Alvy and play it while he sleeps, saying over and over again, You WILL and you CAN rid the world of nuclear weapons. But isn't that something the old Raine would have done?

One day I sat on a bench in the village, and an old woman flumped down beside me, and she was wearing the same kind of black tie shoes Vikey used to wear. "Hi," I said. "Top of the morning to you." She commented on the adorableness of my baby, and how tiny he is, and I said, "That's because he's quite young—not because he's undernourished." It's a pity I have to defend myself like that. Perhaps it's because I am always picturing a social worker with a black briefcase coming to the farm, making her way down the hill toward us, wincing as her high heels sink into the mud, and me running out the back door and dropping Alvy into a tiny boat in the stream, like Yokheved did for Moses. The woman sitting on the bench said she lived on Grove Street. Grove Street, Elm Street, Maple Street—it all sounds so copasetic. I was hoping she'd ask me over for tea, but she didn't, so I felt compelled, very politely, to invite *myself. I promised to bring a cake. She seemed slightly resistant, but I must get to know some of our neighbors and introduce them to Al. He has these terribly clamlike tendencies that the farm does not discourage, and I can see him and me becoming more and more interior, taking our fantasies and building them into two giant acorn academies.*

* *

In the tub, Raine tried to imagine what life felt like before it was thought of, during the fifty million years when there were roses but no humans. She thought of how storms had invented her—the hot seas, the black nights, the cracks of pink lighting, the endless stalking of mortality. She wondered if life was a cataclysm steadily wiping out the old and clearing the way for new creations, or if it was a calm seabed waiting for the next soft element to drop down from the stars.

She tried to remember the days when she was an amphibian—eons spent in the silent seas, when the crust of the planet was cooling and buckling, the mountain spines were shifting, layers of smothered forests were pressed into seams of coal. She could picture those steamy afternoons, evolution building change upon tiny change—scalding seas, undersea mountains of purple lava, silver bubbles of oxygen rising up through deep, hot rock. She could see plankton flashing bits of stored-up sunlight through foggy water, weird creatures living in darkness, starfish and crabs and blue mussels and sea butterflies and fish with blue teeth scouring the bottom for food. She looked down at her reflection in the water and thought of a pilot in a bomber above the purple islands of Japan, flying over a sea full of octopus eggs and twenty-armed starfish and seals resting on sandbars and moon jellies and butterfly fish and red coral and yellow seahorses. She closed her eyes and saw the blue of dissolved minerals, bacteria and algae forming skins and curds, the thrashing tails of cells, thickets of worms, blizzards of white bacteria surging up in hot plumes, molecules tumbling into clusters of cells, the hazy turquoise days when life first began.

* *

Al just took a huge pile of our laundry to the Laundromat, and I watched him going up the hill with this sack of dirty clothes bobbing behind him, and suddenly I realized that I've left too much for him to do. In the city, Mary did everything for me, and then I moved in with Al—which I must admit is a living arrangement I pushed him into—and now he does everything. Alvy and I have become like fleas riding around on somebody's fur coat. I am sure we should move out right away, but where would we go? Mother and Daddy might take us in, but they dislike Alvy and even the thought of Alvy, and much as I've tried to understand their position, I absolutely cannot feel sympathetic. In fact, I am so mad at them that living there isn't really a possibility.

And I love living here and basking in Al's kindness. Mary comes up on her day off, cleans the house, plays with the baby, and makes banana cake for us. Everyone has been so wonderful to Alvy and me. Beginning immediately, I will apologize to Al.

The other day, I walked into the Chickenbone Café, and Russell Schweickart was sitting at a booth in the back, waiting for me. Rectangles of pale rose light were falling onto the tables, coffee was trickling into a pot, bacon was sizzling on the grill. The ceiling was slanted in one direction, and the floor in the other. Pink roosters were printed on the tablecloths, and plastic tulips were stuck into jelly jars. I couldn't believe my eyes—finally, I see my hero! I haven't laid eyes on him since I was eleven. At last I can be involved in a mature relationship. He was a very kind-looking man with white hair and blue eyes. Of course, he informed me that he was married and had six million grandchildren, but I didn't mind because I am more interested in his morality than anything else, and I honestly do not want to be so acquisitive. I was acquisitive with Pavel and where did it get me? (Pregnant, postcards from Israel.) Russell was so nice and I knew he would be—and I remembered being at space camp and learning the five character traits necessary to become an astronaut: bravery, technical skills, scientific curiosity, physical stamina, and a spirit of adventure. I thoroughly admire someone with all those traits but no longer *wish to attempt to be like them. (I've decided that instead I'm going to be who I want to be, not who I am.) Russell seemed to like me, and as we were eating our fried eggs and rye toast, I could not believe I was sitting there with a guy who was such a big dreamer that he catapulted himself to the stars. I believe the two of us think alike, but no one else thinks like us. Yet two people thinking alike seems to be enough. Two people talking to two people talking to two people.*

* *

Al walked into the farmhouse and saw his ironed shirts hanging from the knobs of the cupboards. "What are you doing?" he said.

"Ironing every single thing in the laundry bag," Raine said. "Even your pajamas. Even your socks."

"What's that smell?"

"I made you a meat loaf."

"I thought you didn't believe in cooking cows."

"I don't," she said. "But you believe in eating them." Alvy was asleep in his basket by the window. As she unplugged the iron and put away the ironing board, she sang:

> *Oh, I'm marching off to Trafalgar Square,*
> *I'm marching off to Trafalgar Square!*
> *Dropping bombs is all the rage,*
> *But I'd rather live to a ripe old age!*

She turned to him and smiled. "I had breakfast with Russell Schweickart in the Chickenbone Café," she said.

"Strange things are always happening in Fairyland."

"Stranger things are happening here. I'll be back at St. Ursula's tomorrow. I'll have a long commute. I won't be home until dinner."

"It's okay, Al. I've been in the corral a while. I guess I'm ready for the rodeo."

"I'll watch Alvy Saturdays if you want to work."

She smiled. "You really like me, don't you?"

"Of course," he said.

"How was your visit with Frieda?"

"It was illuminating. I always adored her, and I've realized adoring someone is a very safe thing to do. It doesn't require anything of you or them."

"I should stay home with Alvy and cook him kosher food and read the Torah to him. But I don't know. I really want to be like Esther, who saved her people from destruction. And there's a lot to do. Gandhi said it's easy to wake a sleeping man but it's impossible to wake a man who's pretending to sleep."

Al poured tea into two cups and said, "Raine, I don't mind going back to work. I'm even looking forward to it. But I do not want to spend the day worrying about you and Alvy. Promise me you'll behave."

"I'll try," she said.

From underneath the hutch in the dining room, a cricket was chirping.

Raine placed a jar of blue delphiniums on the table and sat down across from him. "Do you think being sensitive is the same thing as being weak?" she said.

"I don't think you're weak, and I don't think I am either. We've both endured betrayals."

"And we've survived," she said. "And multiplied." She walked over to him and hugged him as he sat in the chair, and he thought of the day in his office, so long ago, when she had placed her hand on his arm.

"You've been really, really, really, *really* nice to me," she said. "You're one of the seventeen trees that hold up the teepee."

"Thank you, Raine."

"People are always trying to smooth out relationships, but in relationships, you have to leave the lumps."

He smiled. She was a confused kid with some cockeyed ideas. She said a lot of crazy, jangling things, but she made him feel serene. Society was suspicious of him—yet all suspicion withered in the strength of his feelings, as all false things must. The world was full of falsities. But Raine was a true thing.

ACKNOWLEDGMENTS

For their encouragement and support, I thank my family, the Hurleys and the Kerns, as well as Kathy Archer, Lisa Bankoff, Bibiana Garcia Bailo, Ellie Byers, Sandy Fitz-Henry, Joseph Gainza, Jane Gelfman, Anne Greene, Aostre Johnson, Noor Jehan Johnson, Judy Kleinberger, Stephen O'Dwyer, Gene Pelzar, Holly Peppe, Melanie Perish, Linda Perry, Heidi Pitlor, Jonathan Radigan, Toni Stone, and K.K. Wilder.

St. Ursula's Girls Against the Atomic Bomb was truly a collaborative project, and I thank the following people for reading and responding to the manuscript: Mamta Chaudhry-Fryer, Sara Beck George, Nora Mitchell, Christopher Noel, Dorothy Nierman, Paul Nierman, Pia Nierman, Kate Nitze, Carol Pelzar, Wes Sanders, Emily Skoler, Meg Smith, Christopher Tebbetts, Wendy Weil, and Susan Young.

I rewrote this book at The MacDowell Colony in March, 2002, and I am deeply grateful to everyone at the colony for creating such a beautiful and wholesome climate in which to write. I also thank the Millay Colony, the Vermont Studio Center, Yaddo, the Lila Wallace-Reader's Digest Fund, the Bailey/Howe Library at the University of Vermont, and the friendly people at Mirabelle's, the Fletcher Free Library, and MacAdam/Cage Publishing for their many kindnesses.

Working with my editor, Anika Streitfeld, has been a privilege and a joy. Anika is a brilliant and exuberant woman, and I am grateful for her kind manner, wonderful ideas, and exacting eye. I thank Beatrice and Irving Kern for orchestrating celebrations and sharing their life wisdom with me, and David Poindexter for believing in my novel.

I also thank those who are not present to share in my happiness: my father, Kendrick James Hurley; my daughter, Mara Elaine Kern; and my grandmother, Anona Marie Straut. Their amazing love abides with me.

Finally, my gratitude to my friend Tom Corcoran for his generous and significant contributions to *St. Ursula's Girls Against the Atomic Bomb*—and to the talented, loving, and remarkable John Alan Kern, Erin Hurley Kern, and Christine Eldred, without whom I could not have written this book.